Jenny, Sam and the Invisible Hildegarde

Original title: Jenny

by MARY KENNEDY

Illustrated by Adrienne Adams

SCHOLASTIC BOOK SERVICES

NEW YORK · TORONTO · LONDON · AUCKLAND · SYDNEY · TOKYO

For
Jim and Foster

Copyright 1954 by Mary Kennedy. All rights reserved. Published by Scholastic Book Services, a division of Scholastic Magazines, Inc.

12 11 10 9 8 7 6 5 4 3 2 1   1   7 8 9/7 0 1 2/8

Contents

Trouble in the Morning

Jenny held her knees very stiff and moved by a series of springing leaps over the hot pavements. Although it was early morning, Jenny felt the midsummer Florida sun burning through her dress and making a round warm spot on top of her head. She whistled and called as she bounced along.

"Here, Sam, Sam! Here, Sam!" But no small brown dog came running to answer her.

When she reached the flat white bridge which led across Narrow River, she stood for a few minutes looking down at the blue water hyacinths floating below. The moist coolness along the riverbank was pleasant, but Jenny could not really enjoy it without Sam.

What could have happened to that dog? As soon as she was dressed she had gone into the yard as usual to say good morning to him, but there had been no sign of him anywhere.

She would look again in the woodshed. Jenny went home quickly with the same swinging gait, slipped down the lane beside her house, and climbed the back fence.

She helped herself over by holding on to the strong scuppernong vines that almost covered an old oak tree just inside the yard. Her dress caught on a nail as she jumped down. She looked at it. It was a small tear, didn't amount to anything.

"Jenny!"

Jenny started up the tree. If she could manage to climb it before Aunt Linda saw her, she would be safe at the top behind the thick vines. She meant to go in as soon as she had looked in the woodshed.

Aunt Linda put her head out of the kitchen window. Her short light brown hair was bright in the sun.

"Jenny, you come in here this instant!" The expression on her thin young face showed that she meant what she said.

Jenny gave up the idea of escape.

"I'm not hungry, Aunt Linda." She curled her bare toes obstinately in the dust.

"Hungry or not, you can't waste good food! Come to breakfast."

Jenny's small freckled nose wrinkled with the effort to find another excuse.

"Did you braid your hair fresh?" her aunt asked suddenly.

"Yes, I did, Aunt Linda." Jenny held out one of her long pigtails so that her aunt could see. "Couldn't I stay out a minute? It's such a lovely morning!"

"Lovely!" said Aunt Linda. "It's a scorcher! Your mind's not on the morning."

Jenny began to laugh. She could never fool Aunt Linda. Aunt Linda laughed, too. Everyone always laughed with Jenny.

"Please, Aunt Linda..."

Aunt Linda looked at her keenly. "It's that dog again," she said, "isn't it?"

"I can't find him, Aunt Linda."

"He can wait. You come on in."

Jenny went in slowly.

"You must help me today. I've promised to finish making over a dress for Miss Simmons from across Narrow River and I can't stop until it's done. We need the money."

Cora Belle and Harry, the twins, were at the table when Jenny sat down. Harry was big for six. He had close-cut flaxen hair and solemn brown eyes. Cora's bright eyes were full of mischief. Her body was thin but her cheeks were round. Harry was eating heartily the hot hominy and milk and molasses in his bowl, but Cora was idly tracing the pattern of the blue lines on the milk pitcher with her spoon.

Aunt Linda put a bowl of cereal before Jenny. Then she poured boiling water into a cup in which she had put a teaspoon of powdered coffee, and sat down beside her niece.

"How do you catch a flying fish?" asked Harry, looking at Jenny.

"You send an angel fish after it," said Jenny.

Cora laughed.

Aunt Linda was thinking of something else. "I heated up the biscuits I made last night. Do you care for one, Jenny?"

Jenny shook her head. "You have them, Aunt Linda." She jumped up and put three biscuits on a plate and offered them to her aunt.

"Thank you, Jenny. I believe I will have one. You take the others." She took a biscuit. "Lovable's fretful this morning. He kept me awake half the night."

Aunt Linda had on a faded blue dress and had

brushed her fair hair into a careless swirl about her face. Her skin was shining from being splashed with cold water, and she wore no make-up. Jenny thought she was beautiful.

"I don't see how I am going to get through this day," she said as if to herself. "Lovable's got me worried. Drink your milk, Cora Belle."

Cora stopped what she was doing and took a sip of milk.

"I've finished. Can I leave?" demanded Harry, slipping off his chair, which had been broken and was mended with heavy wire.

"Careful, don't catch your pants on that wire," warned his mother. Harry wore a pair of cotton cowboy trousers with fringe down the sides. Cora had on a faded pink dress with straps over her shoulders. It was much too small for her, and had been let down by making the straps longer with safety pins.

"What have you got on?" asked her mother, as though seeing her for the first time.

Cora looked down at herself inquiringly.

"She didn't have anything to wear, so I let the straps down," said Jenny, looking at her aunt as though expecting approval.

"Hasn't she anything else?"

Jenny and Cora both said no. "Her other

dresses are in the laundry bag," said Jenny. Jenny's own dress was torn in two places; whether from climbing trees and fences or from the washing machine down the street, Aunt Linda couldn't be sure. It was a red plaid, clean but rough-dried. Aunt Linda had long ago given up trying to find time for ironing any but the most necessary pieces.

"This very day I'll do something about you, Cora Belle," promised her mother. "As soon as ever I finish this dress I am working on. Jenny, you'll have to take the wash to the Automatic."

"Oh, Aunt Linda!" cried Jenny unhappily.

"Look and see if there is a quarter in the elephant," ordered Aunt Linda. The elephant was blue china and had once held a cactus, but after the plant faded, the elephant became a bank for the washing money. Aunt Linda said that the Automatic was their one luxury; when there was no quarter, Aunt Linda washed the clothes in the bathtub.

"I'll get it!" squealed Cora.

"You'll drink your milk," said her mother. "Wait a minute, Harry. Let's have everything clearly understood. This is a hard day ahead and you must all try to be good. Jenny, you do the breakfast dishes and put away the cots."

"Mustn't they help me?" asked Jenny.

"No, I'm going to ask Cora Belle to pick up for me in the other room and keep an eye on Lovable, so's I can really get to work. Harry must go to the store for me and buy a spool of white cotton, number seventy."

"Could I go now?" asked Harry.

"Yes, come with me and I'll give you the money. Mind you don't lose it. And run right back because I'll need you every minute." Aunt Linda was slim and light and swift. She put a hand on Harry's shoulder and they disappeared into the next room. Cora followed them.

Jenny poured Cora's milk into a bowl. She carried it into the yard.

"Here, Sam, here, Sam," she called softly.

She crossed to the low shed built against the fence. It held odds and ends of trash that Aunt Linda thought might come in handy some day, and for which there was no place in the little house. There was a pile of wood also that they used in the iron stove in Aunt Linda's room if it was very cold, but fortunately it is seldom freezing in Florida.

Jenny found Sam behind the woodpile, lying forlornly on a burlap bag. She saw at once that something was wrong with him. His ears drooped and his tail straggled. He was able to make only one small thump with it when Jenny entered the woodshed. His three strong legs seemed as weak as the one he never quite put down. Because of that crooked leg the other children sometimes called him Wobbles, but Jenny never did. She didn't like it either when he answered to that name. "Where do you think you are going?" she would ask. "Sam is your name! Don't you touch that food until they speak to you properly!" But Sam was not always on his dignity. No one seemed to know how Sam had hurt his leg. If Jenny knew, she never told.

"Here's your breakfast, darling," said Jenny, putting the bowl of milk near him. Sam looked at her adoringly, but made no move to drink it. He did not lift his head, but wrinkled his forehead as he raised his eyes to hers.

Jenny was anxious. "Does something hurt you, Sam?" she wanted to know, sitting on an old crate beside him. She reached down and adjusted the burlap sack. Then she stroked his back. "I wish I knew what to do for you. No use asking Aunt Linda. She doesn't understand dogs." Sam seemed to agree. He closed his eyes.

Suddenly Jenny's face glowed with an idea! "I'll get the book!" She ran across the sandy backyard and bounded up the three board steps that led to the cluttered back porch.

Cautiously she peered in an open window. The room was empty, and on the kitchen table were the breakfast dishes just as she had left them a few minutes before. She listened. There was no sound from the other room. If Aunt Linda came out now, she would force her to stay and clean up the kitchen. She made a face at the canvas cots where she and the twins slept. The sheets were tossed and rumpled. She hated to fold and put away those cots. Jenny longed for a room of her own with a real bed, not like the folding sofa in Aunt Linda's room, which was a bed by night but closed up into a sofa by day to make a living room. In *her* house, too, there would be a special place for Sam.

Sam was not allowed in Aunt Linda's room, although he went in from time to time without an invitation. Then Aunt Linda would scold.

"Jenny, here's Sam again! How many times must I tell you not to bring him into the house? I can't do sewing with a puppy chewing up everything. Look what he's done to this sleeve!"

"Aunt Linda, he's just playing. Sam's a good dog!"

"It's hard enough to manage with a household

full of children. Look where he's pulled the stuffing out of the sofa. You'd think a great big girl of nine would have better sense!"

Jenny thought of these things as she leaned in the window and eyed the bedclothes suspiciously. There was a hump in the middle. Had Harry gone for the thread or was he lurking there to catch her? She balanced herself carefully on the window sill, her legs waving as she tossed the sheets with a lean arm. Harry was not there. The bed was empty. With her bare feet she groped to find the porch again. Her foot struck a collection of milk bottles and they tumbled over with a loud crash.

"Is that you, Jenny? What have you broken now?"

Jenny fell through the window upon the cot in a desperate scramble, and threw the bedclothes over herself. A second later Cora came running in. She looked around and called in her shrill voice, "I don't see her anywhere, Mama."

Then Jenny heard Aunt Linda come in and murmur, "That child will be the death of me." She watched with one eye while Aunt Linda began reluctantly to stack the dishes.

The baby wailed.

"Cora Belle, Lovable's awake. See if you can

quiet him while I put the dishes in the sink."

Jenny stretched a cramped arm. Aunt Linda saw the movement. Her eyes snapped and her face grew angry.

"I'll show you, Jenny Jerrard!" She slapped the bundle in the bed with the flat of her hand. Jenny rolled out onto the floor, half laughing, half crying, and jumping to her feet darted around the kitchen just out of reach of her aunt.

"I am going to punish you, Jenny, if it is the last thing I do on earth. No, you are not too big. Go right outside and cut me a switch from the tree."

"Oh, Aunt Linda, I'm sorry."

Her aunt hesitated. "You deserve it. To behave so...today of all days," she said.

At that moment Cora screamed from the other room. "Mama, come quick! The baby's choking." There were confused sounds of sputtering and howling. Aunt Linda rushed through the door.

Jenny followed her aunt stealthily. Aunt Linda was bending over the clothes basket in which the baby slept. "There, there, darling," she murmured gently. She picked up the baby, who with a red face was gasping out his rage. Cora was watching him, fascinated.

Jenny dropped to the linoleum-covered floor

before the ugly old-fashioned chest and wriggled on her stomach until she could see the book that she had hidden there. She pulled it out and shook the dust off. It was a green-covered book, much the worse for wear. Jenny slipped out of the room unobserved.

Back in the woodshed she turned to the page she wanted and read aloud to Sam:

"The Prince set out to find the healing flower that the witch had told him would cure the Princess. It grew in an enchanted garden. It was shaped like a great white butterfly, and at sunrise its fragrance filled all the air." Jenny's eyes sparkled.

"I've seen it, Sam! I know just where it grows, and I'm going right now to get it. You'll be well the minute you smell it!"

She embraced the sober-eyed Sam, slid around the shed, climbed the back fence, and danced down the lane onto the dusty street. Here everything was scrubby and unkempt. There had been no effort to build or grow anything beautiful in Jenny's neighborhood.

She skipped along until she came to the bridge and crossed over into an older and more dignified part of town. Here were the prettiest homes in Clearhope. The way was bordered with ancient oak trees hung with moss, and Jenny walked slowly under them until she came to enormous gates at the end of the avenue. Beyond the gates with their leaves of wrought metal she could catch a glimpse of the river and the glittering glass of greenhouses, and in between, the gardens seemed to shine and shimmer with every color and every flower in the world. A bird was singing. At the end of a curving drive was the pink stone house. It was aloof and mysterious, set apart from the cheerful white wooden houses that most people lived in, but there was something more. Jenny had inquired about it cautiously, and had been told that it was "the King's place." She had several times hung around hoping to see the king, but so far had seen no one except a man digging in the flower beds. The place was enchanted, she was sure, but she did not as yet know the rules which would reveal the secret to her. She knew from the books she had read that there were rules, and that only by the most resolute abiding by them does one find what one is seeking.

As on other days the garden was full of the fragrance of lilies and roses, and there mingled with this the sharp smell of the pennyroyal that her bare feet crushed as she pressed against the iron fence.

Nothing stirred. It was as though all within were deep in a magic sleep. She could see the

bushes sprinkled with delicate white blossoms whose petals looked like so many butterflies, but how could she ever get one?

Then she saw that the gates were unlocked, were, in fact, slightly ajar. Her heart beat faster. She hesitated...she pushed a little. The gate swung away from her, opening wide.

She went in.

The Magic Lily

Jenny stood for an instant at the edge of the garden. The stone palace seemed to sleep. Perhaps she was the only creature left alive on earth! She walked across the fresh grass, and put out a hand to pick the lily to take back and cure Sam. At the same time the thought came to her that if she had a plant of her own, growing in her own backyard, she would then be ready for anything that might happen. She pictured herself touching Harry's feverish cheeks as he tossed upon his cot at midnight, of quieting the baby, restoring to health and soundness the bedridden old woman next door...why, there was no end to the usefulness of magic like that.

She knelt on the grass and began to dig hastily. She had uncovered one of the crooked bulblike roots from which the big leaves and three blossoms sprang, when a hand fell on her shoulder. Terrified, Jenny looked up into the face of a young black man with piercing eyes. He was the man whom she had seen once or twice through the fence, when he was working among the flowers.

"What are you doing here?" The voice was so stern that Jenny could not answer.

"Do you know that you have just destroyed weeks of work?" the young man asked again. "Give that back to me, and run along home." He took his hand from her shoulder and held it out.

Jenny shook the earth off the root and turned a defiant face to him. She put the plant behind her.

His eyes flashed. "Oh, yes, you *must* give it back. Don't you understand that it's a very special plant? Everything growing here," he indicated the flower bed, "all of this group, is part of something important."

"I know it," said Jenny.

"Come then, let me put it back. You wouldn't have any use for a flower like that."

"Oh, yes, I have!" said Jenny.

"It doesn't bloom every year. There may not be

another specimen quite like that in this garden."

"I know it," said Jenny.

He looked at her impatiently. "What if I tell your father and mother about the way you're acting? They'd be ashamed of you!"

"Oh, no, they wouldn't either, because I haven't any!" Jenny answered.

He tried again. "Look at it. Do you see that one of the flowers is wrapped in gauze?"

It was true. One of the buds she held in her hand had a little hood tied over it. Jenny looked at him, wondering, and then saw that a few other blossoms on the bush beside her were tied up in the same way.

"I had to get up before sunrise to put that on, before the insects were out."

"I'll give that one back," said Jenny.

"Don't break it off the stem!" cried the young man. "I don't want the blossom, I want the *seed*."

Jenny didn't say anything, but she put the lily behind her.

He seemed baffled.

"I can't cope with you. You'd better come inside and talk to the chief. Come along."

Jenny didn't move.

"Wouldn't you rather give it back?" he asked.

Jenny shook her head, then turned suddenly

and tried to run, but he seized her braids and she was captured.

"Now into the house with you." Keeping a tight hold on her two braids, he pushed her up the path.

Jenny clung to the flower. It always happened this way in the stories in the green book. A dragon, an ogre, a genie from a bottle...if you were brave they could not defeat you.

The man led her across a patio, with borders of sweet smelling shrubs and low beds of yellow and purple summer flowers.

They entered a silvery hallway from which the house seemed to open out on every side, with windows stretching to the floor and touching the overhang of the sheltering roof. Jenny looked out across the peaceful gardens to the sultry waters of the river. She forgot her fear and the humiliation of being made to go where she had not intended to go. She thought that she would like to sweep down the wide staircase in a gown woven of moonbeams, wearing a crimson and ermine cloak which trailed behind her. She would step into a glass and golden carriage drawn by eight gray horses. She was suddenly aware of her torn plaid dress, her bare feet.

"Let go my hair!" she said. "You churl!" She

spoke as the prince spoke in the book. She had no idea what it meant.

The young man smiled and released his hold. "Then come quietly," he said.

With a rebellious look Jenny moved on. The waxed floor was as smooth as glass. Perhaps it was glass, you couldn't really tell. She would call it glass when she told Harry and Cora about it.

He knocked on a closed door.

"It's Robert," he called. "May I trouble you for a moment, Dr. Oliver?"

"Yes, come in."

Jenny was frightened. What would happen now? Robert opened the door and Jenny saw a man sitting behind a desk. He did not speak, but looked at her with surprise in his calm straightforward eyes. Jenny looked back at him respectfully.

"This child has dug up one of our *Hedychium coronarium*. I've tried to tell her what it is, but she says she knows, and she won't give it back."

Behind the desk long windows were open and Jenny rushed swiftly forward and ran outside. This should be easy! She was used to outrunning Aunt Linda.

"Mind the steps!" called the tall man, springing up, but it was too late, Jenny had already stumbled. She had skinned her knee badly against the stones of the terrace, and thoroughly frightened she began to cry.

He helped her gently to her feet.

Jenny remembered that if one faces difficulties, they disappear. She blinked back the tears.

"No one will hurt you," he said. There were kind lights in his eyes. He looked exactly like a king, except that he wasn't wearing his crown.

"Won't you give me this?" he asked, touching the drooping plant.

She shook her head. "I need it," she said earnestly.

"Then let her keep it, Robert, if she needs it. You go back to your gardening. I'll attend to that scratch on her knee. Come with me," he said and smiled at Jenny. She tried to smile back as she followed him into a wonderful room, all glass and sunshine. The furniture seemed to be of glass, too, and there were shiny tools and jars of many shapes and sizes. Under one jar a blue flame was burning. Near the window a sink held a small tank of seaweed.

He washed her knee with cool water, dabbed something on it with a bit of gauze, and stuck a bandage over the scratch.

"There," he said, "no great harm done."

Jenny leaned back in the chair. She felt suddenly tired, as though she had been running fast in the hot sun.

He half filled a glass with water. "Drink this, you'll feel better," he said.

She fixed her eyes upon his face before she took it. It could be that she would drink it and fall into a deep sleep during which time they would take the lily away from her, or it could be that it was a magic potion which would actually make her feel better. But surely this was really the king. She drank. It was a tasteless drink, but she did feel better.

"What's your name?"

"Jenny Jerrard," she told him. She looked at the lily. It was beginning to turn brown. "It may not be any good now," she murmured faintly.

"Then give it to me, and I'll get you another to take home."

She hesitated. "I'll keep this one until we get to the bush," she decided. "Sam is mighty sick," she explained. "I have to have it for him."

"Who is Sam?"

"Sam is my dog. He won't eat anything, he pants, and his ears droop. He just lies around the woodshed looking mournful. I couldn't do anything for him."

"I see. I see. Well, these are dog days. Perhaps I can give you something which may fix him up." He went over to a cabinet, mixed a yellow powder with something else, wrapped it into two small papers, which he folded and gave to Jenny.

"I don't know much about dogs, but I think if you give him this, he will soon be all right."

"Yes, sir, thank you. You're a good king."

"Don't mention it," he murmured. "Ah... um ... let me know how Sam gets on."

"I will ... if I can," she answered, thinking of Robert.

He seemed to read her thought. "You mustn't mind Robert. His plants and his experiments mean a lot to him, and to me. We hope to find how we can use these green things in many new ways. For instance, you could make paper from that lily you have — and perfume, too." Jenny was not surprised. "Would you like to see our greenhouses some day?"

"Maybe."

"You'll enjoy it. Robert has a green thumb."

"I thought so!" said Jenny, narrowing her eyes. "He didn't like it because I dug up this flower."

"No, he didn't. You see we had that one marked for a hybrid. He was trying to make an even better one. By the way, why were you digging it up?"

"Don't you know?"

"Should I?"

"I reckon you're surprised that I know about your flower, but I've got the book," she said. "I had to have it to cure Sam. I couldn't let him die."

"Oh," he said, as though she had explained everything. "You're sure this is the one?"

"It grows in a king's garden, doesn't it? And it has the fragrance that drifts about the earth at dawn...hasn't it?"

"And you're sure it would cure him?"

"Better than any medicine!" Jenny exclaimed positively. "Just give him a whiff of it! Not that this powder isn't welcome. Is it some witch's brew that only you know the secret of?"

He smiled. "No, Jenny, it isn't magic. I learned about that when I studied medicine, but now I'm a scientist — that's a different kind of a doctor from the ones you may be used to. Part of my work is finding out new things about plants."

"I'm not used to doctors," Jenny said. "Aunt Linda says we can't afford to be sick, so we don't need a doctor most of the time." Actually she had seen only one doctor in her life, the dumpy, busy man who had come the night Lovable was born and shut her in the kitchen with the twins.

She glanced away.

"I thought at first you were the king," she said, disappointed. "Is the king in?"

"I'm Dr. *Oliver* King. You could just call me Dr. Oliver. But, Jenny, that's just my name. We don't have kings in America, you know."

"I know that. But is every place America?"

"What do you mean?"

"Is this place America, and the garden outside, is it America, too?"

"Yes."

"I didn't know that. In books only kings have palaces and gardens like this."

"Can't we be friends anyway? I'd like to be friends with you, Jenny. It gets pretty lonesome around here. I'll tell you what. I have a lot of books that I read when I was a little boy, and some of them I know you'd like. Why don't I lend them to you? You take away all you can carry, and when you've read them bring them back and get more. Would you like that?"

"Oh, yes! Thank you. But *he* won't let me in."

"Robert? He'll let you in, I promise. Come along, I'll get you another flower."

Jenny walked quietly beside Dr. Oliver, holding her head high. She was wearing an exquisite dress that swished around her ankles, and her shoes were purple leather. On her glorious hair was a glorious hat. They had been friends for a lifetime. She had come back here across seven seas to see him...on his birthday...because of that friendship...his wife was her friend, too....

"Have you a wife?" asked Jenny suddenly.

"Jenny, that's a hard question. Yes and no."

"Did she die?" asked Jenny timidly.

He shook his head. "No, she went away."

"For good? Isn't she coming back?" Jenny asked.

He stood looking gloomily across the garden, but he did not answer.

"That's why you're lonesome, I guess," said Jenny practically. She was sorry she had mentioned his wife. She longed to say something that would please him, but she couldn't think of anything.

"Oh, your flower!" he said finally.

"Never mind about the flower," said Jenny, giving him back the plant. "I'd a heap rather have this old powder!"

The Invisible Hildegarde

Sam tried to leap up when Jenny came into the shed, but when she offered him the powder he turned his head away.

"Now, Sam, that's not nice! It will make you well. He said so. Look! Like this! Watch Jenny." She put out a pink tongue and touched an infinitesimal bit of powder which was in the open paper. The taste was not pleasant. She admitted it.

"It's horrid, but it will make you well." She offered it again. Sam looked at it closely and sneezed. Jenny saved the powder just in time. She put a little powder in the palm of her hand and held it out to him. He licked it affectionately, and then cocking one ear, he gazed at her with a pained expression. She put more powder on her hand. Gradually he had taken it all, and tired of her petting and coaxing, twisted around on the burlap bag and by his gesture expressed his determination to get a little rest.

Jenny entered the house fearfully. She had been away half the day, and she was in doubt of her reception. Harry met her.

"Where have you been?" he demanded. "The baby's awful sick," he boasted. "Mama says she never had a baby as sick as he is."

Jenny tiptoed into the other room. Her Aunt Linda looked up from the low chair in which she sat with the baby on her knees. Lovable was wailing weakly.

"I'm awfully sorry, Aunt Linda," began Jenny. She was full of sympathy since her recent worries over Sam. A baby was almost as precious as a dog, she thought generously...for those who cared for babies.

Aunt Linda looked at her sadly. "Thank goodness, you've come at last. Jenny, I'm too tired to scold you. Will you fix something for the twins to eat? There's some cold biscuits and syrup, and some grits you might heat up. Just give them anything you can find. It's getting late. I put away the cots, but I had to leave the dishes."

Jenny looked out the back window.

"Cora! Hoo-hoo, Harry!" she called in guarded tones. "Come in here and get something to eat. Cora Belle — *la!*"

The twins came running.

"Your mama says for you both to come and eat. You can pitch right in and help wash up the dishes while I fix it."

"I'm going to ask Mama if we have to wash dishes," protested Cora.

Jenny grabbed her dress as she started into the next room. "She's putting Lovable to sleep. Don't you dare go in there. Aren't you hungry? I'm going to fix something mighty nice. If you don't want to help me, don't. It just takes that much longer." She began to pile the dishes in the dish pan.

The twins stood watching.

"She *may* not spank you," said Jenny, beating up the suds.

Cora Belle took the dish mop out of Jenny's hand. Jenny smiled at her and threw Harry a dish towel as she moved to the "safe" in the corner and scrutinized the contents through the wire netting with a satisfied air.

"How would you like *delicious* fried hominy and syrup?" she asked.

"All right," replied Harry without enthusiasm.

Jenny put the pan on the kerosene stove. She poured some vegetable oil into the pan and let it get hot. The cold hominy she cut in strips and dropped into the hot oil to brown.

"Just set the table as you dry the dishes," said Jenny. "Now, Harry, do it right. It only takes a minute. Shake the tablecloth out of the window. Don't leave the breakfast crumbs. Shall I tell you what Hildegarde would do?" Her eyes twinkled.

"Oh, yes, please tell us about Hildegarde," Cora begged. "Is she coming to lunch, Jenny? Is she coming to lunch?"

"I haven't decided," said Jenny, sure of their attention, for Hildegarde was the favorite of all the stories that she told the twins.

"Oh, let her come!" urged Harry.

Jenny turned the brown slabs in the pan. "If she smells this cooking, she'll come without being asked. Get the syrup, Cora."

Cora flew to the cupboard and took down the syrup pitcher. It was always kept there with a cup over its nose to keep out the ants.

"You did real well with the dishes, Cora Belle," Jenny praised. "But Hildegarde likes flowers on the table, don't you remember? She has flowers growing in every window of the ash-cans."

"Does she really live in ash-cans?" asked Harry.

"Yes, she has to, it's all she's got, but she has fixed them up simply wonderful. Made little windows and put red geraniums on the outside."

"What'll we use for flowers on the table?"

"I could get some oak leaves," suggested Harry, "from the tree near the back porch."

"The very thing, and bring in a piece of grape vine," said Jenny. "Take down that shiny jar, Cora, and put some water in it. Hurry, Harry!"

Harry climbed the tree by way of the broomstick suspended on two ropes from the lowest

limb. This the children called "the acting bat"; it figured in their circus games, and provided a quick way up and down the tree. Harry snatched a handful of leaves, threw them on the ground, "skinned the cat" on the bar, picked up the leaves, and was back in the kitchen as Jenny put the sizzling food on his plate. Harry thrust the leaves at her.

Cora was pouring syrup liberally on her hominy.

"Stick them in the jar." Harry did, and helped himself to syrup.

Jenny served herself. She was hungry.

"May I have some milk?" asked Cora.

"See how much is left. Your mother has to have some for the baby."

Cora brought the bottle over to the table. They all looked at it.

"You could have a little," Jenny decided.

"Isn't there any condensed milk?" asked Harry. "I'd rather have condensed milk."

"No, there isn't any." She saw the scowl on Harry's face. "Why, look who's here!" cried Jenny. "If it isn't Hildegarde!"

"Where is she?" asked Harry with interest.

"Just coming in the door. *Hello, Hildegarde*, you haven't been here in a long time! How are things in the ash-cans?"

"Make her answer!" ordered Cora. Jenny got up and stood in the doorway. She took a firm stance and turned her elbows out. Her face took on an expression that the twins knew well.

"Hello, everybody," said Jenny.

"Hello, Hildegarde," cried the twins, delighted. "Come and sit down. Would you like some lunch?"

"No, I should say not. I've had mine. Some watermelon rinds. Perfectly delicious."

The twins shrieked. "Did you cook them first, Hildegarde?"

"Not at all," said Hildegarde, taking a chair and putting her elbows on the table. "I swallowed them three at a gulp. I always gulp my meals — saves time."

The twins laughed again.

"Have you a table in the ash-cans?"

"Oh, I've a scrumptious table. I made it out of an automobile tire."

"But, Hildegarde, how can you eat on that? It has a hole in the middle."

"I eat on the edges. Of course I have to use special dishes, so they won't slide off."

"What do you use?"

"I turn everything upside down. Like this," she said. Jenny took a saucer and turned it over.

"You see this little place here on what *you* call the underneath side, that has a little rim around it? That's my dish."

"Oh, I want to eat out of the wrong side of the saucer," cried Cora. "Give me some more, Jenny. Let me try it."

"You can't do that here," said Jenny sharply, becoming herself again. "When she invites you to her house you can use her dishes. And, Hildegarde, we don't put our elbows on the table."

"I'm sure I don't mind if you don't," said Hildegarde. "It doesn't offend me. Behave as you want to in your own home, I say." She beamed upon them, propping her elbows boldly in front of her. The twins laughed with joy.

"How do you get into your house, Hildegarde?" asked Harry.

"It's a secret."

"But you told us last time."

"Then you must never tell. Did I say I crawled in?"

"Yes."

"Well, now don't you repeat this, but sometimes I slide in, so as not to disturb the rugs, you know."

"What rugs? What kind of rugs? What are they made of?"

"Palmettos plaited — and they go right up the sides of the walls to the ceilings, so that I am in a kind of basket. That's one room anyway...the way I have it decorated. It's my bedroom."

"How big is your house, Hildegarde?"

"It has several rooms, all very neat and clean. I can't bear things left around, even in the animals' ash-can."

"How many animals have you now?"

"Oh, dozens. Such darlings, but so talkative! I've had to make the possum live on the roof, because he really does chatter, and I've put the turtles in the window-box with the geraniums. That is, I put them there when it rains. Oh, my goodness, I must be going."

"Oh, don't go, please, you haven't told us..."

"I'll stay long enough to help you with the dishes," said Hildegarde graciously. "*If* you hurry. Cora Belle, you wash and Harry and I will dry. Come on! Quick, quick, get them in the pan! That's what I do." Jenny moved like lightning taking the dishes to the sink. "Jenny can heat the baby's milk, *if* she wants to. Go on, Cora, wash them. Don't wait for me."

Jenny filled the bottle and put it in the kettle to heat. "You finish up the dishes or it will be a long time before Hildegarde comes again," said

Jenny. "And if your mother comes out, don't let her see Hildegarde, and don't you tell her she has been here. Promise."

"I promise," said Harry.

Jenny took the bottle and went into the next room.

"You go and get something to eat, Aunt Linda. I'll take Lovable. I left some hominy in the pan. You must be all worn out."

"I am, Jenny." Her aunt smiled faintly and laid the baby in Jenny's arms. "You can be good when you want to be. Did you have yours?"

"I had all I wanted." Jenny cradled the whimpering baby carelessly in her arms. "Close the door, Aunt Linda. I'll put him to sleep."

She thrust the bottle into the baby's mouth and gathered him up against her, hushing his cries with the warm milk and the comforting accustomed rubber nipple. Jenny rocked him back and forth. He looked up at her with one big round trusting eye. She patted his back gently.

"Sleep, go to sleep, sleep deep, sleep deep," she murmured. The eye closed slowly then opened with a jerk. "Go to sleep, darling. Wake up well," crooned Jenny. The eye fluttered and closed. The baby slept.

Jenny admitted to herself that there were times

when a baby was sweet. She placed him carefully in his basket and entered the kitchen with a self-satisfied air.

"He'll be all right, Aunt Linda. I've put him to sleep."

The baby was better the next day and so was Sam.

Sam frisked to the back porch and devoured a plate of scraps with good appetite. Jenny thought he might enjoy seeing the King's place, so she washed carefully, combed her hair, and set out.

Sam followed, walking unsteadily on his weak paw.

Jenny's Dark Secret

Through the iron gates Jenny saw Robert stripping moss from a magnolia tree.

"There he is, Sam!" she whispered. "Do you think we could sneak past?" She chewed a finger. "Maybe Dr. Oliver didn't mean it. I reckon we'd better not go in."

Robert looked up at that moment and came towards them. "Hi!" he called.

"Run like everything, Sam," advised Jenny, as she fled down the street, but Sam was staring at a grasshopper. Jenny stopped. "Come on, Sam. Here, Sam! Come on, Crazy!"

"The doctor wants to see you," called Robert.

"I'll come tomorrow," said Jenny.

"No, now. The doctor told me to tell you that you are welcome any time."

Robert opened the gates wide, and Jenny marched in, followed by Sam who showed a great interest in everything.

"You are welcome as far as I am concerned, too." Robert added. "That is, as long as you don't dig up the lilies."

"Of course I won't," answered Jenny indignantly.

"I'm relieved to hear it," said Robert. He led the way around the side of the house.

"I'm sorry I gave so much trouble," said Jenny stiffly. "It was to save a life."

"Oh, yes," said Robert. "The doctor explained that to me."

"But I was wrong," admitted Jenny.

"Never mind. I've replanted it in a pot in the greenhouse and I think it may grow again."

Jenny didn't answer. She had already said that she was sorry and she saw no reason to overdo it.

They went up the steps of the terrace to the long windows of the room that Jenny had been in the day before. Dr. Oliver looked up from his microscope when they came in.

"Well, hello!"

Jenny was suddenly shy. "This is my dog, this

is Sam," she said. "We came to thank you for the medicine. It cured him," she added.

"Good," said Dr. Oliver. "Come in and sit down. So, this is Sam." He lifted the little dog and stroked him lovingly. Then he moved the feeble paw gently back and forth and stretched it out.

Jenny watched him with a dark look on her face. The chair she was sitting in was very comfortable, big and soft, but she could not enjoy it.

"I won't hurt him," said the doctor, seating himself near her. "How did he do this?" he asked.

She looked at him with a startled expression. He waited for her answer, his eyes on hers.

The color flamed in her face. She could feel her cheeks burning and her eyes filled with tears.

"I did it," she sobbed. "I did it!"

It was the first time she had told anybody and it made her feel better, although she saw the shocked light leap into the kind eyes opposite, and that made her feel ashamed.

"*You* did? How?"

"It was when he was just a little thing...a little tiny puppy, and I was sweeping the porch. I didn't want to sweep it, but Aunt Linda made me. She put the broom in my hands and she told me to do it or I'd be punished. I was awfully mad,

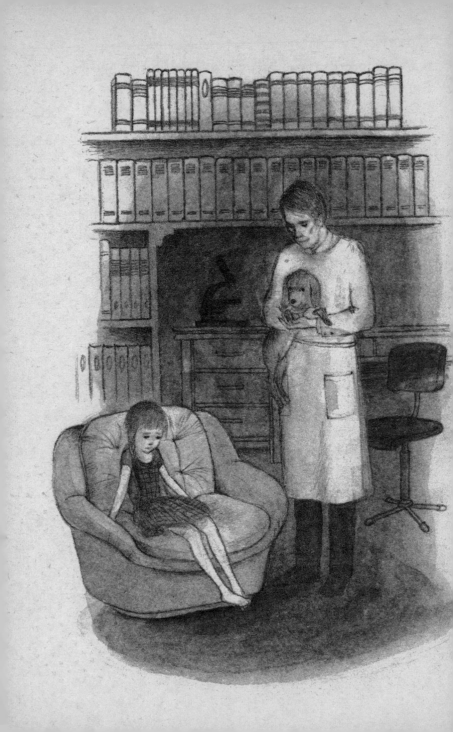

and Sam kept running in my way, and chewing at the broom. I shouted at him. I said, 'You behave now!' But he wouldn't, and I swept him off the porch!" She cried harder and her face felt like nothing but lumps, and her heart felt like a lump, too, because she was so sorry she had done it, and she wished that she could go back to that minute and not do it...not sweep him off the porch, but pet him, and love him and put him gently aside.

"Well, then what?" he asked quietly as though he knew that was not all.

"He cried. Then he crawled off with his leg dragging, and he was squealing and moaning, and nobody helped him at all. I didn't help him because I didn't know what to do. I got down and looked under the porch, and he was moving around in the dirt and biting at his leg. When he saw me looking at him he just crawled away, as though he hated the sight of me. Now, you'll hate me, too!"

She kept her eyes on the floor but she wasn't crying any more.

"No, I don't hate you," he said. "We all do terrible things when we lose our tempers."

She nodded. "I try not to get mad like that now."

"That's good. So do I."

"*You* do? Did you ever do anything you wish you hadn't?"

"Oh, yes, Jenny, many times. Once I hurt someone I loved very much."

"Sam forgave me when he saw how sorry I was, and I've made up my mind not to be mean or angry any more. I try to stop it when I see it coming."

"I wish it were as simple as that," he murmured.

Jenny turned to see what he was looking at, but there was nothing. Just some flowers on a table in the sun.

"Dr. Oliver, was the person you hurt so bad, the one you told me about...that went away?"

"Yes, Jenny."

"Maybe she will forgive you the way Sam did me?"

He patted her hand. "Come along," he said cheerfully, "we'll have a glass of milk together and then I'll give you the books I promised."

On the way home Jenny and Sam stopped in the empty lot on the corner. She wandered about happily picking wild flowers. Some grew low, spreading webbed stars on the grass. There were big bushes of coarse lantana, a few fragrant shrubs, and a gigantic bush of wire weed, the pointed white brushes sticking straight up on top. A flowering vine straggled over fallen bricks. Jenny added the fringed blossom to the flowers whose stems felt hot in her fist. Sam nosed about in a spasm of joy, finally hopping around in wider and wider circles with his nose to the ground. He would not come when Jenny called and she walked down the street without him.

When she had gone about a block, she stopped and whistled for him, at the same time admiring the pretty house in front of her. It was one of her favorites. It had pale blue awnings, and window boxes full of white petunias. There was a vine of white mermaid roses over the front door, a lantern hung at the side, and flagstones led around the house into the garden. It was half screened by tall flowering shrubs, and through them Jenny could see a man moving back and forth at his work. She heard the buzz and click of the lawn mower. Through an open window she caught a glimpse of blue walls, pale curtains, and gaily flowered chairs. She wondered who lived there.

A taxi drew up at the curb. Few taxis were ever seen in Clearhope; they came from the next town where there was an airport and a railroad station.

The driver began piling suitcases on the sidewalk. There were small bright labels pasted on them, with pictures of mountains, and lions, and wings. Jenny tried to read the printed words: London, Roma, Paris, and Hotel. Then the driver opened the door of the cab, took out a hat box and a small square bag. A young woman stepped out.

Oh, to be like that, thought Jenny. To be just like that! To have lovely sad dark eyes and hollows in the cheeks...and to seem as if you didn't care a bit how beautiful you were. As she stood against the green background, she made Jenny think of a butterfly lily.

In her arms was a small cream-colored Pekinese. It nestled against her, and fixed bright button eyes on Jenny.

Where has she been? Jenny wondered.

The taxi man tossed a big wool coat on top of the luggage. She must have been far away to need a coat like that!

The man who had been cutting the grass in the garden rushed out to greet her.

"Hello, Leroy, how nice to see you," she said, smiling as she saw him. Jenny liked her voice.

"Why, Miss Clare, we didn't expect you for another month!" he exclaimed.

"I just got homesick for everybody," she said. "I'm glad to be home," she added. She glanced around and drew in her breath as if she were really glad.

"Maisie will be surprised," said the man called Leroy. "She's not expecting you at all."

The traveler opened a big purse and handed the driver a bill. She waved him away as he tried to give her change. "That's all right," she said.

The driver thanked her. "Shall I help you with these?" he asked.

"We can manage," she murmured.

"How was Europe, Miss Clare?" asked the grass-cutting man as he gathered up some of the bags under his arms and swung two more from his hands.

Europe! Why, that was across the ocean, Jenny realized with a shock. She had never, to her knowledge, looked upon anyone who had been across the ocean.

"Beautiful," Miss Clare was saying, "but it's nice to be home."

The taxi drove off. Leroy started up to the front door, and at that instant Sam appeared. The Pekinese lifted its head, gave a sharp snort, and stared at Sam over a flat disdainful nose. Sam, barking sharply, rushed around Miss Clare to get a better view. The Pekinese struggled to get down and fell to the ground in a wild leap; straightway mistaking itself for a lion, it took up a brave position beside the luggage.

Leroy set down the bags he was carrying and

ran back. He shouted to Jenny, "Call off that yaller dog!" Then he stood helpless as they chased each other in and out of the luggage. Sam ran between his feet and circled Miss Clare.

"He's a *brown* dog!" said Jenny. She crooked her elbow threateningly and made a fist. Her eyes were half closed and her upper lip thrust forward. She had seen little boys do that trying to defend themselves from bullying, but it only lasted a moment, for there was something — was it laughter? — in Miss Clare's face that told her it made her look either ugly or funny, and Jenny didn't want to be either.

"Well, call off your brown cur," roared Leroy.

"Leroy!" Miss Clare reproved, then called coaxingly to the little Pekinese, "Come, Delilah. Here, Delilah! Could you help us?" she asked Jenny.

"Sam, come here!" shouted Jenny over the din. She put the book and the flowers down on the sidewalk, and going up to the dogs laid a determined hand on Sam.The barking and growling continued, but Sam backed away. The Pekinese gave a few shrill yaps and stared at him scornfully.

The front door flew open. Jenny caught a glimpse of someone standing there, as Miss Clare snatched up Delilah. She gave Jenny a smile and a grateful nod as she ran into the house.

Leroy was grumbling as he loaded himself with bags. "Why don't you leave that mutt at home?" he asked rudely.

Jenny was about to answer back when she remembered what she had told Dr. Oliver that morning. Because she remembered, she wasn't even angry. Without a word she picked Sam up and walked away leaving Leroy astonished. She did not even glance at him. It was rather funny.

She stroked Sam. "Good boy," she said. "Come along with Jenny. I like you better than if you had a longer tail!"

She was filling a jelly glass with water when Aunt Linda came into the kitchen. Jenny had hidden the book she had borrowed on the shelf in the corner near the cots.

"Don't splash the floor," said Aunt Linda. "I just scrubbed it. I wish you wouldn't bring those weeds into the house. They don't last a minute and they shed all over everything."

Jenny obediently started off to the woodshed, walking slowly and carefully toward the door with her hands clasped about the jar of wild flowers.

"Just weeds," repeated her aunt.

Jenny raised reproachful eyes. "Why, Aunt Linda," she said, "I think weeds are wonderful."

Aunt Linda came out on the back porch and called after her, "Jenny, come right back in here with that red plaid dress. I want to mend it before you go to the Automatic. You didn't take the clothes when I told you to, so you'll just have to go now. Better hurry or they will be closed."

Jenny left the flowers in the woodshed and ran back to the house.

She stepped out of her dress, pulled a few sandspurs off the hem, and handed it to Aunt Linda. Her aunt turned it over and made a little clicking sound. She threaded a needle.

"This needs a patch. Look in the scrap bag and see what you can find." She sewed up the smaller tear easily. You could hardly tell where it had been torn. Jenny gave her a bit of cloth. She measured it against the hole and nodded.

"Put something on, Jenny. Don't stand around like that."

"I haven't anything else, have I? — except my good polka dot. My other two dresses are in the laundry bag."

"Try on that tan cotton blouse of mine. It's too small for me."

Jenny put it on. "It fits me, Aunt Linda."

"Well...it's not too bad. Isn't there an old wash skirt hanging on the hook? Yes, that's the one. Bring it here." She took it in firm hands, measured Jenny with her eye, and tore a foot of cloth off the bottom. Then she split it down the side, reached out for Jenny, pulled her nearer, and wrapped the skirt around the small waist. She tore a width out of it. Then she went to the machine, hemmed up the bottom and the sides, and put it on the child.

"Why, it looks just fine, Aunt Linda. I've got a real wrap-around."

"It'll do for now. It will get you to the Automatic and back. But don't you wear it again without asking me. I haven't the time to fix it properly. Now run to the laundry. Put in the red plaid."

Jenny took the big bag down the street. Business was slow, so the manager turned on the washing machine while she waited.

A baby sat quietly in the middle of the floor playing with a cat. Jenny tried to coax the cat away from the baby. It was a big lazy cat with a white ruff under his soft face. He touched Jenny's hand with a friendly paw. The baby began to whimper. Jenny walked away from them both.

The machine stopped. The man opened the enameled door, and tossed the newly washed clothes into a clean bag. Jenny handed him the quarter.

Then she took the damp clothes home, and she and Aunt Linda hung them up on the line.

Jenny was glad that she would have a clean dress to wear next day. She smoothed out her dresses as she pinned them up, so that they would dry without wrinkles. Then she stretched Cora Belle's and Aunt Linda's things the same way.

"Thank you, Jenny," said Aunt Linda with a sigh.

Hope

Jenny read the book she had borrowed, as soon as
it was light, before even the baby woke up. She
had tumbled out of bed and into her clothes,
which she had arranged carefully on a chair when
she went to bed, so that she could step into both
dress and panties at the same instant.

She washed her face, brushed her teeth, and
gave her hair what Aunt Linda called a lick and a
promise. Then she took the book and climbed to
the top of the oak tree. In this private castle of
green air, hidden by moss and the wandering
grape vine, Jenny did most of her reading. She
heard the calls below when breakfast was ready

but she finished the last few pages before she climbed down.

When she went to return the book, Dr. Oliver seemed happy to see her. He suggested that it might be a good day to go through the greenhouses.

Robert was busy with some small plants and black earth, but he stopped what he was doing when he saw them.

"Will you show us around?" Dr. Oliver asked him.

Robert looked pleased. "You don't mind if your dog waits outside, do you?" he asked Jenny. Sam was already in, but he followed Robert back through the open door. Robert patted his head, spoke a few words to him, called him old fellow, and Sam sat down in perfect understanding to wait. "That's a smart animal," said Robert to Jenny who was watching gratefully.

Inside the greenhouse the filtered light gave everything a special quality, almost as though they were moving in clear water. It was sweet and moist there, of a different temperature from outside. Everywhere Jenny looked, a new color glowed, and the air was full of alluring scents.

"Here we pay no attention to the seasons," Robert said. "If the conditions are right, the flower just has to bloom when we ask it to."

He picked three small blossoms and held them out to her.

"*Pink* violets!" exclaimed Jenny, astonished.

"Yes, *Rosetta*. They are very fragrant. Those blue ones are called *Marie Louise*."

He lifted a small pot with a sprouting vine in it. It had curious spear-shaped leaves widely spaced on a yellow stem.

"You haven't seen this in some days, Dr. Oliver," he said. "It's coming along nicely." Then he showed it to Jenny.

His face had such a rapt expression on it that she looked from him to the plant and then back again. It was as though he held a jewel in his hands.

"That was a seed which came from an Egyptian tomb," Dr. Oliver told her.

"The seed may have lain there for two thousand years, and it still had life to grow," said Robert. He put the little vine in a safe place. "It is not like any plant I've ever seen," he added.

They walked under trees of flowering mimosa that reached almost to the glass roof and seemed to send down showers of gold. There were enormous white daffodils nearby. Robert said the bulbs had been flown to them from Ireland.

"You must see my herbs," said Dr. Oliver, leading the way into a smaller greenhouse.

It was a beautiful spot, crowded with many banks of growing plants, some covered with small flowers. The air seemed full of hanging baskets trailing delicate foliage. Dr. Oliver introduced Jenny to some of the plants, giving her a leaf now and then, crushed between his fingers, so that she might smell the delicious warm oily fragrances.

"These are the great herbs," he said, repeating the names for her. "Mint, lavender, basil, sweet marjoram, balm, bergamot, sage, hyssop, rue, spike vervain. And that big fellow in the corner belongs with them. That's lovage, and it can grow six feet high." Then he added, "You will notice, Jenny, that I say 'urb' in the ancient way while Robert and the English say 'herb.'" His face seemed to shine as he looked around.

The two men began to talk earnestly together. The long names of plants rose and fell in the air. Jenny tried to read the names written on the wooden labels thrust into the earth near each plant. Some were very difficult.

"I'd like to know the name of every single flower in here!" cried Jenny.

Dr. Oliver's approving eyes made Jenny feel as though she had said something clever. "In time...all in good time," he said.

He touched the shaggy trembling leaves of one of the plants. The leaves drew up quickly and folded together. "See, Jenny, when you poke it, how it closes up. It is called the Sensitive Plant. Some people are like that..."

Jenny tried to spell out the label on the plant.

"Never mind the Latin names for a while, Jenny," Dr. Oliver advised. "The English names are so beautiful, and are full of meaning. Know the flowers by sight and perfume. That's enough for most people. Look about you and enjoy yourself."

Robert had stopped before a flat box of seedlings. "This is my version of one of Dr. Carver's experiments," he said proudly.

"Who is Dr. Carver?" inquired Jenny.

"You never heard of *Dr. Carver?*" Robert asked. "Dr. George Washington Carver, who did so much for the South...for farmers everywhere?"

Jenny shook her head.

"She has heard of him now," said Dr. Oliver, chuckling. "He was the son of a slave and became a great scientist, Jenny. He discovered how to make hundreds of new products out of peanuts and sweet potatoes, and found wonderful uses for common plants, and did many other things. I have a book about him you can borrow, if you like."

"My Uncle Henry could grow things," Jenny volunteered. "He grew vegetables in our backyard. He planted some muskmelons, too. They were better than you can buy in the store. Simply delicious! He put pepper and salt on them, at least he used to," she explained, "before he went away." Perhaps Uncle Henry had changed.

They were walking back the way they had come, but along a different side of the greenhouse, and they came to the orchids growing in moss. Jenny stopped and stared. She had never imagined anything to equal the splendor of the jungle blossoms. Fantastic winged forms that seemed to be made of silk, or velvet, or wax, in colors she had never seen.

"Robert makes quite a tidy sum out of that collection," Dr. Oliver said, as Jenny stood entranced before them. "He enriches the world while he enriches himself."

"An orchid is very slow-growing," Robert told Jenny. "It takes almost a year just for the plant to produce the seed, and about eight years, all told, for the blossom. I figure that you earn anything you are willing to wait for."

"Did you know, Jenny, that vanilla comes from an orchid?"

"It does? I didn't know that," Jenny said in wonder.

"One that is a native of Florida." Dr. Oliver

pointed it out; it had a strange pod like a capsule. Further on, Jenny noticed some plants with many of their blossoms tied up in gauze hoods, just like the hood she had seen on the lily. Dr. Oliver explained that Robert had crossed the flower with another, different one. He had put the pollen on the flower, and when he planted the new seed it would be something more beautiful or more useful than the old one.

When they stepped outside the greenhouse the heat of the day came back upon them like a wave. Sam was waiting patiently. Dr. Oliver lifted him in his arms.

"You were a very good little dog," he said. He looked at the leg again. "Jenny, while you are selecting another book I want to take a picture of this leg."

"Why?" she asked, alarmed.

"I want an X-ray. Do you know what that is?"

"No."

"It is a picture that shows the inside of a person. This one will show me the bone. I'll let you look at it when I take it. Oh, Jenny, while I think of it, come any time and read the books whether I am here or not. The door is always open, and you may ask Miss Nelson, my assistant, for anything you want."

"I thought I'd cut some roses for this child to

take home with her, Dr. Oliver," suggested Robert.

"I'm sure she'd like that. Wouldn't you, Jenny?"

"Oh, yes, I would!" Jenny exclaimed, looking across at the rose garden.

"Then come up to the house when you have finished, and find a book." The doctor strode off. Sam yelped as he left, as though to ask Jenny: "Is it all right for me to be carried off like this, and leave you behind?"

Robert cut the roses carefully with his pocket shears. He told her the names of the ones she liked best. "These are all prize roses," he said. "The best have gone, but the Pink Radiance is pretty now."

"I may have a garden just like this some day when I grow up," Jenny told him. "And a greenhouse, too!"

"That's nice," Robert said politely, going on with his work. But he looked up when Jenny confided, "I think Dr. Oliver is just wonderful!"

"So do I," he said. "Everybody likes Dr. Oliver. He's always doing something for somebody. He sent *me* to Hampton College, and helped me to get my diploma from Agricultural College, too."

"My Aunt Linda got a diploma from High School. When I grow bigger I'm going to get a diploma, too. Aunt Linda says it's a very useful thing to have."

"It is a useful thing." He sounded sure. "You'd better go right along to college."

"Oh, I will," said Jenny. "My Aunt Linda was going to college, only she got married instead."

Jenny looked along the triple rows of the rose garden which stretched straight to a wreathed pergola. Then she examined a bright green bug glowing like a jewel on a rose petal.

"I wish Dr. Oliver was happy," she said.

"Well, perhaps he's not unhappy," said Robert. "But I'd say he was a very lonely man...very lonely."

"I guess he misses his wife," said Jenny wisely.

"He does," said Robert, lowering his voice. "But he never mentions her."

"He did to me," said Jenny. "Where is she?"

Robert turned away and snipped off a rose.

"Oh, far away," he answered. "Over the hills and far away."

"You're just saying that!" exclaimed Jenny, looking at the flat land stretching away into the distance.

"Now he works too hard. He works all the time.

That's not right, you know. I guess he needs a woman to take him in hand."

"Do you mean that when he was married he didn't work so hard?" asked Jenny, puzzled. "My Uncle Henry worked harder after he was married than he did before. That was how we lost him. Aunt Linda says he just couldn't stand any more."

"Did he die?"

"No. He went away. We don't know where he is."

"Doesn't he write?"

"No. He wrote one letter when he left." Her voice was lost in the sound of water as Robert filled a pail at a nearby spigot.

"I'll put the roses in this bucket just inside the greenhouse door," he said, "and you can take them with you when you go."

Jenny went back to the house, to the room where the books were.

She found some wonderful ones. There were story books and picture books, histories, geographies, books about animals, and many books about flowers. There was poetry, too. Jenny thought she might write a poem to Dr. Oliver. She thought about it a long time, but she couldn't exactly begin, so she put it off to another day. She decided to ask if she couldn't take one of the picture books to the twins. She would first read all the books with big print. Jenny thought she would like to read as many books as possible while she was permitted to come and go like this. In her experience, good things did not always last. Then she forgot everything. Forgot even where she was, in the joy of that library.

When she came out, Dr. Oliver was standing at the window looking at some strange dark squares. "The X-rays," he explained. "Sit down," he said and then, just as though she were a grown-up caller, "I'll be with you in a minute." He went back to the squares.

Jenny was very quiet. She couldn't guess what was in his mind. She wondered where Sam was.

A door opened, and Miss Nelson came in. "Will you need the dog any more, Doctor?" she asked.

"No, you may let him out. You met my assistant, Jenny, didn't you?"

"Hello there," said Miss Nelson and almost smiled. She went out quickly and quietly. In a moment Sam came hobbling in and lay down at Jenny's feet. She waited. It was pleasant there. She enjoyed the peaceful room and the long windows, and the way the sun came in, and the radiant colors from the garden that seemed to dance in the air.

"Jenny," said the doctor finally, "I'd like to try

to do something for that leg of Sam's."

She looked up at him. "You mean fix Sam's leg?" she asked faintly.

"I couldn't promise to fix it, but I could try. There is a chance that I could help him."

"Oh, Dr. Oliver!" Jenny could scarcely breathe.

"I'd have to keep him here for a while, of course. It would take time to heal, and you must understand, Jenny, that I am not sure it will do any good, but if you want me to, we could give it a try."

"We could give it a try," she echoed, gazing at him adoringly.

"I'll get a vet to give the anesthetic."

"A soldier?" asked Jenny who knew the word.

"Not exactly. A veterinarian. A doctor of dogs."

"Oh!" said Jenny.

"Then could you be here tomorrow, with Sam, say at nine o'clock? I'll try to have everything set up."

The next morning Miss Nelson was waiting for Jenny.

"Stay right here until you are called. They want to wash the dog," she said.

"He may not like it," said Jenny.

"Come on, Sam," said Miss Nelson.

Sam looked at her gravely and did not stir.

"Don't let's keep them waiting," said Miss Nelson. "Tell him to come."

Jenny picked Sam up and carried him through the door. "Where do you want him?" she asked.

Everything happened quickly. Dr. Oliver took Sam and handed him to another man in a white coat, who had a bath and towels all ready. Miss Nelson drew Jenny away immediately. She led her into a bathroom and told her to wash her face. Jenny did.

"You're a nice-looking child," said Miss Nelson. "I like your braids." She took a new comb out of a cellophane wrapper and smoothed a few stray hairs back. "Does it take you long to plait them?"

"Not very. I'm going to get me some ribbons some day soon."

Miss Nelson handed her a towel. "Wash your hands and scrub your nails with that little brush there."

"Why must I get so slicked up?"

"Because you are going into an operating room. You have to help keep Sam quiet until they put him to sleep. He won't be frightened if you are there. But you know, Jenny, it's fun to scrub up every day, anyway. If I give you that little brush, will you use it all the time?"

"I might," said Jenny.

"All right, it's yours. You may have that little comb, too. It's nice to carry in your pocket. You've got a pocket, haven't you?"

Jenny nodded. Miss Nelson dried the nail brush on the towel and gave it to her. Jenny slipped both things into her pocket. "You're like my Aunt Linda," she said. "Aunt Linda says it doesn't cost anything to wash."

"I'd like her, I think. The world has many wise people, it seems."

"But Dr. Oliver is the most wonderful of all, isn't he?"

"There's nobody like him. He's the kindest man I've ever known," agreed Miss Nelson. "He's a fine scientist, and could have been a great surgeon. I suppose you realize that he is taking time for this from very important work?"

"Oh! No, I didn't," answered Jenny, feeling happy.

Sam was sitting wrapped in a bath towel on a snow-white table under a blinding light. He gave a sharp bark when he saw Jenny.

"Speak to him and tell him he is all right," said the strange doctor. "Explain what we are going to do."

"Lie down, honey," said Jenny to Sam. "We are going to cure your leg. Look at all the trouble everybody's taking for you, just to try to make you well." She smoothed his head. Sam struggled to get off the table. Jenny held him firmly. He quieted, looking at her obediently.

The doctor passed a cloth before his nose two or three times. It had a heavy, sweet smell.

"Don't get too near, Jenny," said Dr. Oliver.

Jenny murmured comfortingly. Sam settled down. Then the doctor held a cone-shaped cup of cloth just above Sam and poured a few drops of the sickly sweet stuff on it. Every time he poured a drop or two he brought the cloth nearer and nearer to Sam's nose. Sam was falling asleep, and then suddenly he *was* asleep.

Dr. Oliver nodded to Miss Nelson and she drew Jenny away. "Can't I stay?" begged Jenny in a whisper.

Miss Nelson frowned and put her fingers to her lips. When they were in the outer room and the door shut behind them, she said, "You'd better go home, Jenny, because Sam will have to stay quiet when he wakes up; it will be a day or two before we know anything."

"I...I...don't want to go home now. I'd like to wait."

"They need me in there, so I have to go back.

Better not wait, dear. It may be a long time. Be a good girl. I suppose you could come back this afternoon. Not too early, though."

Jenny went slowly, hardly noticing where she was going. She turned off Green Street and walked a block or two down to Narrow River.

The cool damp sand felt delicious between her toes, as she waded in the shallows under the trees, stepping now and then over the huge roots of a cypress. She flushed a white heron from the weedy edge of the river, and it sprang up and soared majestically away. A fish jumped out of the water, it was a big mullet. Then a kingfisher flew about, crossing and recrossing her path, a gleam of sapphire plunging and darting over the still water. A big turtle slid from a log with a gentle splash as she passed. There were many butterflies, that seemed to fall out of the sky one by one, floating about her lazily as she went along; yellow-white they were.

Jenny looked up. There was a vulture in the distance, high on a gaunt palm tree, his hard eyes searching the clean waters. Aunt Linda had told them that the vultures were useful in the forest; they kept it clean and orderly, but they were so ugly they made her shiver. She looked away. The river was lined with yellow lilies and water lettuce. She could not wade there, so she walked in the dry white sand further up the bank, following the river as it twisted and turned, and dreamed.

Two fishermen were sitting in a small boat beside the far bank, patiently waiting for their lines to tighten.

Jenny began to wonder where she was. She stood for a minute listening to the water that lapped the white sand with a laughing sound. The smell of woods and loam and fishiness was strong and bracing in the warmth of a fair day. The sky through the tangled branches was burning blue. At that moment in the lofty stillness she knew that everything would be all right with Sam, so now she thought that she had better go home.

She scrambled up the bank and came out at a point just beyond the edge of town. She turned back in the direction she had come, and running and leaping was soon at a corner she knew, and from there went on back to Green Street.

Delilah

Jenny had forgotten to take the roses that Robert had cut for her the day before, and wondered if they were still where he had left them, thrust to their necks in a bucket of water. She decided that she would go by and see, for she would be sorry to hurt Robert's feelings and besides, if she took them home, they might forestall questions about Sam.

They were still there, just inside the door. Jenny reached in, took them up, and shook the water from them. The drops stood darkly upon the white dust.

"Let me give you some fresh roses," said Robert, stepping out of the greenhouse, shears in hand.

"Oh, I hate to waste these!" Jenny exclaimed, regretting that she had forgotten them.

"I'll find a use for them," said Robert. "Let them be."

Jenny watched while he cut a fresh armful for her.

He dampened some newspaper and wrapped up the stems. "These will be all right," he said, "although I've cut them at the wrong time of day."

"They are beautiful, beautiful!" said Jenny.

"They do well," said Robert, "but the best of them have passed."

Jenny carried them carefully.

"Where on earth did you get roses?" asked Aunt Linda. Her face wore a soft expression that Jenny seldom saw. Once in a while she looked at the baby with the same sort of smile, but never at Jenny or the twins. "Why, they would cost you seven dollars in a florist's shop," added Aunt Linda in delight.

"Could we sell them?" asked Jenny. She knew the value of money.

"It is much easier to buy than to sell." Aunt

Linda's voice was bitter. She had sold most of her meager possessions. "Who gave you these?" she asked suddenly.

Jenny was vague. "The gardener at one of those places on Green Street. They've got big glass houses there, and flowers to waste."

"I don't know why you go wandering around Green Street," said Aunt Linda. "Get me that big pitcher to put these in."

"It's so pretty there," said Jenny, filling the pitcher at the sink.

"Well, be that as it may be, you keep an eye on the twins today, and take them with you. Better just go to the park. See that their faces are clean."

"Oh, Aunt Linda!"

"Don't you 'Oh, Aunt Linda' me! I've got to go and try a blouse on a new customer. I've let down a skirt for her, too, and I must return it, and get the money today! I'll take the baby with me — it's not far, and I like him to get the air, but the twins are your responsibility and don't you forget it."

Jenny said nothing. She did not want to tell Cora Belle and Harry about Sam, and she knew she had to think of some way of going back to Dr. Oliver's without them. Aunt Linda went into the sitting room with the roses, and Jenny could hear the whirr-whirr of the sewing machine. Lovable slept in his laundry basket on the back porch, covered with a green mosquito netting. Cora and Harry were in the far corner of the yard playing some muddy game. They had a few bottles filled with water ranged along the crosspiece of the fence, and from time to time poured a little water into an old pan, stirring sand into a mud pie.

Jenny had forgotten to bring home the books she had selected the day before. She had time to read, but no book, and so the golden moment was lost. It was seldom that she had no task hanging over her head. But today Aunt Linda had folded up the cots, washed the dishes, and swept the floor. Jenny sat in the kitchen window and looked out. A bluejay pecked at something on the big tree. It flew off in a flash of blue.

"Jenny!" It was Aunt Linda. Jenny never answered the first time she was called. There was always a chance that something else would claim Aunt Linda's attention and she might not have to go at all.

"Jenny!"

Jenny didn't move. "Yes'm," she answered.

"Come here, please. Don't wake the baby." The machine resumed its whirring sound.

Jenny went in to the front room. Aunt Linda had placed the roses where she could look at them while she worked.

"There is just nothing at all to eat in the house," she said. "Go see if you can find anything we can give the twins. Are you hungry?"

"Not very," said Jenny, but she was.

"I'll get some money this afternoon. I've been pinched all week."

Jenny looked the larder over. There was a little rice in the bottom of a can. She put it on the table. Two soda biscuits, half a cup of dried cowpeas in an old coffee tin, a dab of margarine. That was all. Then she thought of something. What had she knocked off the shelf the other night when she hid her book? She recalled the sound now; something heavy. It had fallen behind the set of drawers that stood under the shelves and held pots and pans and groceries. Jenny tried to peek behind it. It stood away from the wall but it was difficult to get at. The cots were rolled into the corner out of the way until night. Jenny got the broom. She moved it back and forth behind the chest of drawers until it struck something. Jenny squeezed herself against the wall, thrust an arm into the opening. Her fingers touched a round object. A can? It might be a cup, of course.

She used the broom again. Out it came...a can of spaghetti.

She rushed into the other room, her hands behind her back. "Aunt Linda, I give you three guesses!"

"Now, Jenny, don't do me that way. Tell me what it is."

Jenny brought out the can triumphantly.

"Why, where on earth did it come from? It's just like an answer to a prayer."

Jenny heated the spaghetti. She laid the cellophane mats on the table and a fork by each plate. Her rule was never to use anything extra, and thus she saved dishwashing. She bustled into the next room. "Everything's ready, Aunt Linda. I'm going to put the roses on the table." Then she thrust her head out of the window and called to the twins, "Come and get your dinner while it's hot," she ordered. There was a face towel hanging on the rack with the dish towels. This Jenny dampened under the tap, and as Harry came through the door she seized him and wiped his face. He screwed it up unhappily, Jenny gave him a push. "Go and wash those dirty hands." She wet the other end of the towel. "Come on, Cora Belle. You can smell the roses while you eat."

Cora spread her hands out and looked at them. "I'm not very dirty," she remarked complacently.

"Says you." Jenny scrubbed a streak of brown mud from the untroubled forehead. "Go wash your hands."

"Harry, hold your plate." She ladled out the spaghetti.

Harry tasted it and murmured with pleasure.

Aunt Linda came out. She, too, held her plate near the kerosene stove while Jenny served her from the pot.

"Everybody can have half a cracker," said Jenny. "Aunt Linda, could we use the paper napkins?"

"I don't see why not," said Aunt Linda graciously. "This is a regular feast. We may as well be stylish."

Cora and Harry wanted to go back to their game as soon as they had finished. It took all the wiles and blandishments of Jenny and Hildegarde combined to get any help with the dishes.

Aunt Linda went into the bathroom to get ready to go out, and Jenny could hear the water running and splashing and Aunt Linda humming. The bathroom, which was on the edge of the porch, had been put on as an afterthought. It was roughly boarded in, but it had a tub, a toilet, and a basin. There was also a crazed mirror. The flooring was warped, and you could see the ground beneath through the cracks.

"You look so sweet," Jenny said when she came out, and indeed Aunt Linda seemed another person. Bathed, her hair neat, her lips red, dressed in a thin print dress of soft rose and yellow, bought off a marked-down rack in the best department store, Jenny thought she looked just as well as any woman on Green Street. "I love those colors," said Jenny.

"It's awfully old, but it's the only thing I own," said Aunt Linda. "It surely was a bargain: cheaper than I could buy the material. This wonderful country! If you can just get hold of a little money, there are plenty of bargains. No wonder fine dressmaking is dying out. If it weren't for Lovable I'd take a secretary's course."

"Don't you have to pay to study that?" asked Jenny, who had heard her say this before.

Aunt Linda smiled. "I mean I'd take it if I had the money and the time. Do you think I ought to wear my hat?"

"I haven't any hat," said Cora Belle.

Her mother laughed. "Be glad of it," she said. "Then you have no problem."

"It's a mighty nice hat," said Jenny, "but lots of people don't seem to wear any."

"I'm going to the other side of the river, perhaps I'd better." She went into her room and put it on.

"I never knew Lovable to sleep so long," she said. "I guess I can't take him, Jenny. You children will just have to play around the yard."

"Oh, no, Aunt Linda!" moaned Jenny.

Aunt Linda grew instantly cross. "Don't you let me catch you running out and leaving the baby. I never know where to lay my hands on you. You dash off somewhere in the morning and leave me to wash up and do everything else. How can I get my sewing done if I have to do all the cleaning and cooking besides? Now, not another word. I've told you what to do." She wrapped up the blouse and skirt.

"Have you seen my measuring tape?" she called, but no one answered. Cora and Harry had gone back to their game, and Jenny was out on the back porch shaking the baby to wake him up.

It did wake him. He had slept long and was rested. He woke with a smile and lay there lazily.

"Never mind!" called Aunt Linda. "I've found it." She came out on the porch.

"Now be good. I'll be back soon. I have to shop,

so expect me when you see me." She raised her voice. "Cora Belle. Harry. You mind Jenny while I'm gone."

"Lovable's awake," said Jenny.

"That's all right. You could put him in his cart and keep him out of doors if you want to."

"Aren't you going to take him?"

"It's too late now."

"I'll help change him."

Aunt Linda hesitated. "Well, don't make such a face! I guess you'll have your hands full with the twins. You fixed lunch mighty nice. I'll take him but we'll have to hurry."

Jenny rushed for a clean diaper, and Aunt Linda snatched a sun suit off the line. Lovable's face was washed with a special towel that hung handily just inside the doorway of the bathroom. Jenny put a pillow in the baby cart and wheeled it to the sidewalk. Thankfully she saw Aunt Linda depart. She went down to the end of the yard.

"Let's go to the park," she suggested.

"I doan wanna," Harry mumbled. He had a scrap of red cloth and he was forcing it into a bottle half filled with sand.

Jenny went into the woodshed. She looked about to see if she had any treasures which she might use as bribes. There were some empty spools, a bit of lace, several enchanted pebbles: one that looked like a bird's egg, it was so smooth and white, and another shaped like a heart, a brown one, flat as a biscuit...no, there wasn't one that she could bear to part with, unless everything else failed. A blue marble. She slipped that into her pocket with the lace.

"Want this?" she asked Harry carelessly, offering the marble. He took it. "What do you say?"

"Thanks." He didn't stop his game.

Cora was interested. Jenny held out the scrap of lace.

"What's it good for?" she asked.

Jenny thought. "Use it for your doll."

"I've lost my doll. Where's Wobbles?"

"Who?"

"I mean Sam. Where's Sam?"

Jenny had been dreading this question, but as long as it had not come in front of Aunt Linda no harm was done.

"He's er..." Jenny did not tell lies. She had discovered that *one could say nothing* in a crisis. She smiled mysteriously, and quickly changed the subject.

"Hildegarde sent you a message," she said. "She told me she was almost sure to be on Green Street this afternoon."

Harry stopped shaking the bottle. This was a game worth playing. Cora stood with her eyes fixed on Jenny.

"What time?" she asked. Cora had a practical streak.

"Oh, any time. All afternoon."

"What's she doing there?"

"She wants to plant a garden around the ash-cans, and she is looking for ideas."

The twins with bright faces waited for Jenny to speak again.

"She thinks she'll put a wisteria around the front door, won't that be pretty?"

"Why doesn't she plant a tomato vine?" asked Harry.

"A good idea," said Jenny. "You must tell her. Let's go find her. She may have the monkey with her."

"A monkey! Has Hildegarde got a monkey?"

"Yes, and it's so *bad*. If it gets into one of those houses on Green Street, it might do as much damage as Lovable."

They enjoyed that, for Lovable had a strong hand and broke everything in his crawling path.

"Let's go," coaxed Jenny.

"Why can't you tell her to come here, Jenny? Make her come here and play with us."

"You know how she has notions," said Jenny, "and this afternoon she has taken a notion to Green Street. I may have to go into one of the houses and see if she is there, while you wait at the gate."

"You wouldn't dare," said Cora.

"Yes, I would. You'll see." Cora Belle was wearing a new dress her mother had made out of one that Jenny had outgrown. "You look nice in that dress, Cora Belle. Come on. Hildegarde said to walk through the park."

In the park, near the lake, they came upon a lost dog. It was wandering along disconsolately and its feet were muddy from the lake's edge. It was a small cream-colored animal and Jenny recognized it at once. She tried to catch it but it bounded away from her.

"I know that dog," she told the twins. "I know the house it belongs to. Help me to catch it. We'll take it back." She was trying to recall what its name was. Suddenly she remembered. They had the dog partly cornered, between a bench, the lake, and the twins. She knelt down.

"Don't move," she cautioned, "and grab it if it tries to run past you. Come, doggie, come here. I won't hurt you. *Delilah!* Come here, Delilah!"

Delilah, hearing her name, came slowly to

Jenny. Jenny seized her, held her securely. She knew the way of dogs. "There now, poor little thing!" She stroked her. "I'll take you home." She lifted the Pekinese in triumph and strode out of the park, the amazed twins trotting at her heels.

Jenny Takes Tea
on Green Street

"We'll go right up to the front door and ring the bell," said Jenny. "Aren't those flowers gorgeous?"

They heard the bell peal through the house, but no one came. They gathered hopefully beside the door which was half hidden in oleanders. On one side there was an emptiness of sky edged with trees, beyond which, Jenny knew, lay the river.

The mocking birds whistled and sang. Other birds chirped gaily. Their wings flashed in and out past the glossy leaves of the camellias and into the fresh green of the beech tree. A sprinkler flung a glittering spray into the sunny air, a clump of zinnias glowed magenta and pink in the round bed beneath the falling water, the ribbon grass curled stiffly beside the mimosa. It shone very white in the direct sun, the tiny green stripes had vanished in brightness.

Jenny saw a brass knocker. She beat it loudly. "They'll be here," she said, but still no one came. Jenny drooped. "I reckon we should go to the back," she admitted. Just then there were footsteps and the door opened. A young woman, cool as frost, with lawn ruffles on dress and apron, looked at them rather forbiddingly, until she saw the dog.

"Oh, you've found Delilah! Give her to me, and thank you very much." She held out her hands.

Jenny did not give up easily. She wanted to see the inside of that house, and show it to the twins.

"May I see the lady of the house?" she asked with dignity.

"Miss Clare? I'll ask. She'll want to thank you. She thinks a lot of Delilah!" She beckoned agreeably and they stepped into the hall.

The maid went upstairs. No sooner was she out of sight than Jenny tiptoed to the door of the living room and looked in.

"Not as nice as my ash-cans," she said in Hildegarde's voice.

The twins were merry. "Oh, Hildegarde, when

did you get here?" they asked, crowding up to Jenny.

"Ssh!" she cautioned with an anxious look at the stairs. "You must both help me make Hildegarde behave." Then with a flash of laughter she added in Hildegarde's voice, "Do you think I could tie my monkey to that table leg? He'll be good unless he gets lonesome, then he'll just eat up the table leg and come and find me, wrapped in one of those yellow curtains like a sultan."

At that moment Harry discovered that by standing on a footstool and hurling himself onto the nearest rug he could slide for a considerable distance over the polished floor.

"You and Hildegarde had better be careful, Harry. You'll hurt yourselves," advised Jenny, straightening the rug. The maid came back. They turned in some confusion.

"Just follow me," she said pleasantly, and led the way upstairs. Cora Belle and Harry were so close to Jenny that Cora's toes grazed her heels from time to time.

At the top of the stairs was a pleasant sitting room, with wide doors opening onto a veranda. It was full of color and sunshine. Fresh flowers, books, and pictures gave it a cozy look.

"Here's Delilah, Miss Clare," the maid announced. "This little girl found her."

Miss Clare laid aside the book she was reading, and came towards the three children who had stopped in the doorway and were staring at her. She smiled at them. Her eyes were not so sad today, Jenny thought, gazing at her with admiration.

"How wonderful that you have found Delilah! How can I thank you, dear?" Miss Clare exclaimed.

Jenny stepped forward and put the disheveled Delilah into her arms. She liked being called dear. She thought again that she would be just like Miss Clare when she grew up. She was fascinated by the way she moved, the way she spoke, the pale colors she wore, and the curious beauty of the thin face shadowed by mournful eyes.

"What a state she's in!" said Miss Clare as Delilah licked her hands and began leaping up to get at her face. "No, no, Delilah, you must have a bath first. Poor little thing, she has had a bad time, and she's glad to be home. I know that feeling. Come in. Come in, all of you, and sit down. Maisie will bring some cookies. Would you care for tea?"

Jenny said she would. She had never tasted tea and she thought that she would like to.

"What's your name, dear?"

"Jenny. Jenny Jerrard."

"Who are your friends?"

"They're not friends. They're my cousins. They're twins. That's Cora Belle, and that's Harry. His real name's Henry, the same as his father."

"It is not," said Harry. Since his father had left them, he had not wanted to resemble him in any way. He was angry when anyone called him Henry.

"Will you have tea with us?" Miss Clare asked the twins.

"No, thank you," they said with one voice. They hadn't Jenny's curiosity.

"Then some milk, perhaps?"

"That'll be all right," said Harry.

"Cora Belle?"

"If you please," whispered Cora. She sat gingerly on a chair near the door.

"You hear, Maisie! Tea for Miss Jenny Jerrard and milk for the twins, please."

Maisie went out and Miss Clare took Delilah over to a basket that was fitted with a mattress, almost like a doll's bed. It had a rubber bone tied to the side and other toys scattered about. Delilah snuggled down, apparently content to be home again.

"Come and sit here," said Miss Clare to Jenny.

"Take that comfortable chair."

Jenny obeyed.

"I suppose you saw the advertisement in the paper...I mean about Delilah?"

"No, ma'am," answered Jenny. "I found her in the park."

"But how did you know where she belonged?"

"I remembered where she lived, because of the other day when you were coming home and I had my dog."

"I think you're a smart little girl, and now I remember you, too!"

"She didn't want to be found at first, but when I called her Delilah she came right to me...didn't she?" She looked at Cora and Harry. Cora agreed, but Harry had screwed around in his chair and was studying the pictures hanging on the wall behind him.

"You knew her name after hearing it once? That was remarkable!"

Jenny glowed.

Maisie brought in a tray with hot tea, two cups, a plate of bread and butter, and some little cakes with chocolate and orange icing. There was a flower in a small vase on the tray. Jenny felt that she and Miss Clare liked the same things.

"I thought I'd fix the milk and cookies downstairs," Maisie said, and the twins jumped up happily.

"I'm sure they'll enjoy that," said Miss Clare. "Be sure that they have some of these little cakes." She offered them the bread and butter. "Will you begin with this, Henry, or wait for the cookies?" she asked.

"Harry!" he corrected, glaring at her.

"Harry. I'm sorry. And you, Cora Belle?"

Each of the twins took a piece of bread and butter. They saw Maisie waiting for them and followed her out of the room.

Miss Clare offered the bread and butter to Jenny. Jenny shook her head. She was too excited to eat. Perhaps there was some special way to eat it. She wasn't sure that she knew. She would wait and watch.

Miss Clare poured a cup of tea. "Cream and sugar?" she inquired.

"Yes, thank you," said Jenny.

Miss Clare handed her the cup and poured tea for herself. She sipped it. Jenny sipped hers. She thought tea a delicious drink.

Miss Clare pushed aside the books on the table. "Put your cup down there, and have some of these cakes. They are homemade." She spread a small linen napkin on Jenny's knee and gave her a pink and white plate. "I'll put them here, and you may help yourself." She crossed the room to a desk near the window, opened a drawer and took a bill from a leather purse.

"I want to give you this, Jenny," she said, offering her the bill.

"What for?" asked Jenny.

"In the paper I advertised a reward."

"But that is five dollars!" said Jenny in astonishment.

"I am so happy to give it to you. You can't possibly know how worried I was."

"Oh, yes, I do," said Jenny. "If anything happened to Sam, I'd want to die. Sam is my dog."

"I knew we had a great deal in common," said Miss Clare gravely. "Take the money," she ordered. "Put it carefully in your pocket. Wait a minute. Let's pin it in. Now, Jenny, you have done so much for me, that I'd like to do something for you. Think hard and tell me your dearest wish."

Jenny thought.

"Isn't there something you wish for?"

"If I had a wishing ring, you mean?"

"Yes."

"Well, I'd wish for Sam to get his leg straight again."

"Your dog has a bad leg?"

"Yes, but the doctor is going to make it all right. He put Sam to sleep, and when he wakes up his leg will be cured, just like in the Bible."

"Is there nothing else you want?" Miss Clare asked.

"That's all. Of course I'd like for us to have a bigger house to live in. Aunt Linda says the country is mighty nice."

"Well, my wish," Miss Clare said, "is that we should have a party together, just you and I. Would you care to go for a ride with me one day, and we'll plan something to do?"

"Oh, yes, I would. Miss Clare, could we go to a circus?"

"Have you ever been to óne?"

"Only to part of one. I saw the parade. Harry got inside the tent, but when they found he didn't have a ticket, they threw him out, and Aunt Linda spanked him, because it wasn't honest, and he could get stepped on by elephants in a place like that!"

"I'm afraid there isn't a circus just now, but when one comes to town again, I'll take you and the twins, too. Would you like to see a moving picture?"

"Well, I have seen one or two, but Aunt Linda

doesn't want us to go unless she knows something about it...even if we had the money. She says it puts ideas into our heads."

"I see."

"But I get my ideas out of books."

"Does your Aunt Linda go to the movies?"

"No'm. She has a baby and she sews for a living, so she doesn't get out much. But she *has* been. When Uncle Henry was courting her, she went right often, she says."

"Doesn't he take her now?"

"Oh, he isn't here anymore. He's gone away."

"How do you happen to be living with your aunt?"

"Because I'm an orphan, so my aunt takes care of me."

Miss Clare said, "What a nice woman she must be! Jenny, I'm an orphan, too. I haven't anyone of my own."

"Haven't you a husband even?" asked Jenny.

Miss Clare was startled. Her hand shook and a drop or two of tea splashed into the saucer. She put the cup down. "Yes, I have, but he isn't with me. His work...keeps him away from me."

Jenny wondered if she should say that she was sorry. She felt shy.

"Well, that's enough about me — let's get back

to the party," Miss Clare said. "We could go to the theatre! There is a summer company, about twenty miles away, that I hear is very good. What are they playing?" Her voice trailed away as she tried to remember. She took a card from a pigeonhole in the desk. "Oh, yes, Gilbert and Sullivan. *Iolanthe*. Music and dancing. I believe you'd like it and your aunt would approve, I think."

"I'd love it," said Jenny.

"Then we'll go. A week from Thursday. Not tomorrow, but next week. Will you come here, or do you want me to fetch you?"

"I'll come here. I'll be over this way anyhow to see Sam."

"Your dog? Where is he?"

"I told you he's having his leg fixed. Dr. Oliver is trying to cure him. He lives in the big house and has all those special plants."

Miss Clare looked as though her feelings were hurt. Jenny wondered what she had said.

Then Miss Clare spoke as if she hadn't looked that way. "I know. I know where it is. It's good of him to help your dog. I might have known. It's so like him."

"Oh, do you know Dr. Oliver?" Jenny was surprised. Then, without waiting for an answer, she chattered on.

"I guess Dr. Oliver is the best man in the world. Better than George Washington, or — or Dr. George Washington Carver. I'm going there now to see if Sam is getting better."

Having thought of Sam, Jenny knew that it was time to go.

"I had a lovely time," said Jenny.

The Windfall

Jenny found the twins sitting on the stone step at the front door. Maisie had put them outside the minute they finished their milk and cookies. They were blissfully enjoying the life of the garden. The glittering spray of water, a procession of tiny ants walking the edge of the very stone they sat on, a caterpillar with a tiger face on a low branch near Cora, and a dragonfly that jerked stiffly through the flower beds. Following Harry's eyes, Jenny, too, saw the dragonfly, blue as a peacock, a toy of gleaming metal that flew towards her without fear. It looked at her from its big dull eyes, lying for a moment upon the air...a miracle of motion that did not move at all! Then it darted away.

"Her ants are just like ours," remarked Cora, rising from the step to follow Jenny.

Jenny led them along Green Street, paying no attention to their chatter. At the great iron gates she paused.

"Do you remember those roses that I brought home?" she asked. "They came from in there."

The twins swung on the iron fence and stared greedily at the garden.

"Who gave them to you?" asked Harry.

"You'll see. Wait right here, I'm going in. I mean Hildegarde is going in. She'll take the turtle and the monkey. And Cloudy, her big cat, will run up the path before her. Won't they be surprised to see her and all those animals?"

"Do you think the animals will behave, Jenny?"

"They might. I'll tell you when I come back. Don't you move from here, now. If you get tired, sit on the grass." She started to go through the gate.

Cora Belle caught her skirt. "Oh, Jenny! you aren't *really* going in there? Oh, don't you dare!"

"When Hildegarde wants to be invisible...she is invisible," said Jenny. "Don't worry about me."

She ran up the path and pushed open the door of the doctor's study. Miss Nelson was there.

"How is he? How is Sam?" asked Jenny.

"He came out of it very nicely. Of course, it's too soon to tell yet, the doctor explained that to you."

"Yes. Is he in?"

"I'm afraid he's very busy."

Doctor Oliver stuck his head out the door. "Is that you, Jenny? Come in and speak to Sam. Mind you don't pick him up." He held out a hand to her. Jenny put her hand in his.

A place had been made for Sam out of a wooden packing case lined with sheets. He was deliriously happy to see Jenny, and licked the hand she held down to him. He could not get up, because his leg was bound on a pair of enormous splints.

"He's coming along," said the doctor, "but we can't be sure whether his leg will be better or not. You understand that, Jenny?"

She knew what he meant. "I forgot my book," she said. "May I get it?"

"Of course."

"May I borrow a picture book for the twins?"

"Certainly. Have anything you fancy. I'm sorry I am so busy today."

Miss Nelson went with her to get the books. The one she had been reading was just where she had left it, and she knew the very one she would take to show the twins.

"Come tomorrow," said Miss Nelson, smoothing Jenny's hair back from her forehead. "You do him good."

"Sam?"

"All of us."

The twins were breathless with astonishment at the sight of the books.

"Mind you don't get it dirty," said Jenny, giving a book to Cora to carry, "because I'll have to return it. Hildegarde's monkey borrowed it. That reminds me, where is the turtle? Heavens! He's still in the book-room reading the books!"

It was almost dark, but there were no lights on when they approached their house. The big oaks draped in gray moss gave the rickety cottage a desolate, almost a deserted look.

The kitchen had a dismal air. Usually, at this time, Aunt Linda had a kettle boiling. Then it was the work of an instant to throw a cupful of rice or cereal into a pot with two cups of water measured into it, and supper was ready in a few minutes. Even Cora could do that much, although she sometimes forgot the salt.

Jenny put the kettle on and turned the flame low. They would most likely have cereal tonight, for Aunt Linda would bring milk from the store. They might even have an egg. In that case, rice, also. She knew there would be some sort of a surprise, too, perhaps a plum apiece, a banana, some figs, or a pear.

Jenny thought she heard a sound from the other room. She went in.

Aunt Linda was sitting beside the sewing machine, her face glimmering sorrowfully through the dusk. Lovable was in his basket.

"Why, Aunt Linda, what's the matter? Are you crying?"

"Well, maybe I am, Jenny. I don't know whether to cry or get mad. I'm just sitting here thinking."

"Shall I turn on the lights?"

'Wait a minute."

"What happened?"

"She didn't pay me. That's what happened. And I haven't a red cent. I just don't know what we are going to do. There isn't a thing to eat!"

"Why didn't she pay you?"

"She wasn't at home. I guess she just forgot that she told me to come. What am I going to do, Jenny? Some people are so inconsiderate. She might have known I'd be counting on her paying me."

"Did you pray?" asked Jenny. Her eyes were dancing in the dark and her fingers were on the five-dollar bill pinned in her pocket. She could imagine Aunt Linda's face when she gave it to her. This was the moment of moments, when things turned out the way they should.

"Of course, I've been praying, but I seem to have all the blackness tonight. I suppose God is sick of me, because I'm always asking for help, and I manage so badly."

"You manage wonderful, Aunt Linda. Please let me turn on the light. I want to show you something."

"Go ahead. But no foolishness tonight, Jenny. I'm not equal to any of your games."

Jenny turned the lights on and unpinned the bill.

"Three guesses, Aunt Linda."

"Jenny, didn't I say I wouldn't play games?"

"Then look, Aunt Linda. Here. Take it. It's for you!"

"But — my goodness! Where did this come from? I can't believe my eyes. My prayer is answered! Where did you get it? Stop that dancing and tell me."

"It's a reward. I found a lady's dog and she gave me that."

"What do you know? I'm so glad to have it, Jenny, but don't think you were paid for being honest, because nobody owes you anything for that!"

"I know. I told her to never mind, but she just *made* me take it. Aren't you glad? She was lovely, Aunt Linda!"

"Well, I'll run to the corner and get something for supper before the store closes. I saw some beautiful fresh vegetables as I passed by. I'm going to give you a kiss, Jenny. You surely have a heart of gold. Keep an eye on Lovable while I'm gone, and if he wakes up, change him. I hope he's not sick, sleeping so much today." She went out into the dark.

Jenny ran to the porch and called after her.

"Get some plums, Aunt Linda."

Aunt Linda's Day
in the Country

On Sunday Aunt Linda did the cooking. She always liked to have a proper dinner on Sundays. "Everyone should be able to count on at least one full meal a week," she said. She cooked because she didn't work on that day. The sewing machine was covered up and pushed against the wall.

After everything was on the stove she rolled out some cookies.

"What are they for? Is it my birthday?" asked Cora Belle.

"No. They are to go with the surprise I am planning for dessert." Her eyes shone mysteriously and she took down a big bowl and began to cut up oranges and bananas. Every once in a while she would sprinkle a layer of coconut.

"Is this the surprise?" asked Harry, enthralled.

"No, this is for our supper. I'm getting it ready now to save work. Once, when I was a little girl, I asked the name of it. They said, 'Lay-overs-to catch-meddlers.' I didn't find out until I was grown that its real name is Ambrosia." She covered the bowl carefully and put it in the wire-netted cupboard.

The children hurried to set the table because of the surprise. Harry drew some pictures and colored them with crayons. He turned the plates over and put one under each plate. He drew a dog for Jenny. He drew a house for his mother because she was always wishing for a better house. He was tired by the time he got to Cora, so he drew some wavy lines for the sea. Jenny put a big leaf from the grapevine on each plate and some leaves and green grapes in the middle with the ketchup and the salt and pepper.

"My, aren't we fancy?" smiled Aunt Linda. She lifted her plate. "What can this be? Isn't it pretty? Is it a boat?"

"No, it's a house. It's a new house for you."

"Oh, thank you, Harry, but you haven't put the country around it. My new house is going to be in the country, with grass and birds and brooks and cows."

"I'm afraid of cows," said Cora.

"So am I," said her mother, "but they look nice in the country!"

"Good luck to me!" cried Harry suddenly, pointing to a broken spot on the edge of his bowl.

"Let me see," said his mother. "Yes, sure enough, Harry has the white bird with the chip out of it."

"You'll get your wish," said Jenny.

"He gets that bowl all the time. It isn't fair," pouted Cora Belle.

"I'll wish that we'll both get our wish," Harry told her generously.

He and Cora Belle shut their eyes and wished.

"Now eat your soup," said his mother. "There's lots more to come."

Jenny had nearly finished hers. It was the best soup in the world, she thought. For two hours it had simmered on the stove, giving off whiffs of inviting fragrance. It was full of vegetables, for Aunt Linda bought a "soup bunch" from the grocer, and that meant one of everything — tomato, potato, onion, celery, squash, beet. If there was any soup left, they would have it tomorrow with another soup bunch added. It became a deeper red in color and was, if anything, more delicious the second day.

After the soup they had rice with thick cheese

melted on top, and carrots cooked whole, and okra.

Aunt Linda looked at the purple seeds of the okra on her plate. "Isn't that a beautiful color?" she asked dreamily. "You remember the prize I won for designing a dress in the Home Economics course when I was in High School?"

Jenny loved to hear about this. She fastened her eyes attentively on Aunt Linda's face.

"Well, the silk I used for the dress I designed was about the color of an okra seed. A sort of pale violet. It was superb if I do say it."

"Will you design my wedding dress, Aunt Linda?"

"Oh, of course I will! I'll start thinking about it right away," Aunt Linda teased.

Jenny blushed. "I mean it, Aunt Linda."

"I'd do better to design some clothes for all of you right now to wear to church. All three of you need clothes terribly. It doesn't seem right to keep you from church and Sunday School because you haven't anything to wear."

"I've got my polka dot."

"Yes, maybe I should have made you go with me today, bare legs, no hat and all. I'll try to do better. I hope to lay a little by during this month to get you some new things to start school with."

"Am I going to school?" asked Cora Belle.

"Yes. This year you'll begin."

"Harry, too?"

"Harry certainly. I'm going to make you a darling dress, Cora Belle, and I'll make Harry a shirt out of the same material."

"I hope in school they teach me how to make money," said Harry.

"Well, I do, too," said his mother. "That would be worth learning."

"May I have some more rice?" asked Jenny, "Lots of cheese, Aunt Linda."

Aunt Linda served her. "Save room for the surprise."

"I'm ready for my surprise," said Cora, pushing her plate away. Her mother put it firmly back in front of her."

"Sit up, dear. I tell you what you do. Take down the tall glasses from the shelf for me."

Cora did. Jenny hastily gobbled the last morsel of cheese. She took the plates to the sink. Aunt Linda was mixing it up in a jar and poured the mixture into tall glasses.

"Ice cream soda," she announced. "There isn't any ice cream today, but I have straws for everyone." She put two straws into each glass.

The faces were all smiles. Jenny tasted hers.

"Oh, my, that's good."

"And a cookie," urged Aunt Linda. "Eat all you want."

"I'd like another!" said Cora. "Is there more ice cream soda, too?"

"A little," said her mother. "When our ship comes in, we'll have real ice cream in it."

For a long time Aunt Linda had been promising them an afternoon in the country and so, as soon as everything was tidy, they set out. They walked the two blocks to the bus happily and quickly and stood patiently for ten minutes waiting for it. When it came, Jenny took charge of Lovable's folded cart, Aunt Linda carried Lovable, and Harry handed the fares to the motorman. There were not enough seats and Aunt Linda said that Harry must stand. "Like a little man," she said. Harry stood, pouting and glum, clinging to the edge of his mother's seat. As they neared the end of the line the passengers thinned out and soon they had the bus nearly to themselves. Aunt Linda's spirits were high.

"These people that you are going to meet," she told them, "were friends of my mother and father. Their name is Harrison. They'll be so surprised to see us! They have been begging me for ever so long to come out and bring you children."

They reached the end of the line and got off the bus. They watched it turn around and go back.

Jenny felt rather lost for a moment in the grove of pine which closed in on all sides. Aunt Linda had inquired about the time of the return buses which ran, the motorman said, every half hour.

"How far is it to the Harrisons'?" asked Jenny."

"I'm afraid it is nearly a mile,"said Aunt Linda, "but it's an interesting walk. There is a short cut, but we might get lost. We had better stick to the road. Mr. Harrison has an old car — a funny old car they call the Rabbit. I'm sure he'd have met us if I'd told him we were coming. Perhaps he'll ride us back to the bus stop."

She put Lovable in his cart and the children followed her as she set off briskly down the road. The cart rolled all right on the pine needles that had fallen thickly everywhere, even over the little used road.

"Why does he call it the Rabbit?" asked Cora.

"Oh, because it jumps when it goes." She made a springing motion in the air with her strong shapely hand.

The children laughed. Lovable looked around and laughed, too, as though he understood.

"Hello, sweet child," said his mother. "Oh, Jenny, I forgot to bring a bottle for him. How could I have been so stupid?"

"I put it in," said Jenny. "It's wrapped in wax paper right in the pocket with his clean diapers."

"Oh, you're wonderful. Thank you, Jenny." She patted the pocket on the back of the cart as if to reassure herself by feeling the bump the bottle made.

On either hand grew the perpendicular pines. Far back from the road placid cows stood plunged to the knees in palmettos, searching for nourishment with bent heads, not knowing that they were lost, not knowing that somewhere through these woods children with eyes as brown and clear as the quiet woodland streams ran and called, seeking them, following the faint tinkling of cowbells and trodden wild flowers.

The white sand of the road grew deeper and Aunt Linda saw that she could not push the frail cart through it. She picked Lovable up in her arms.

"So little and so good!" she said in the special voice she used for him. She stroked his sunny hair, straight and soft, his silken baby hair. The half pout of Lovable's lips broke quickly into dimples.

"If Cora and Harry will take the cart, you and I could make a seat for Lovable, couldn't we, Aunt Linda?"

"Do you think we could make him understand? Let's try."

Each clasped her own wrist and then the wrist of the other. Lovable was already on his mother's arms and clinging to her neck. Aunt Linda shifted his weight. "Come here, Cora, and put Lov-

able's arm around Jenny's neck," said her mother.

Cora did and Lovable was content to leave it so for a little and they walked easily forward with the child enthroned between them, but then Lovable withdrew his arm suddenly after about ten minutes and nearly tumbled off. "I'll tote him a while," decided Aunt Linda.

"Are we nearly there?" asked Cora, stumbling and dragging the cart with little help from Harry.

The pines had thinned out now and there was water in the ditches. Cypresses grew there and Harry was looking for turtles. Aunt Linda had a wary eye out for snakes.

"Just about. There it is yonder."

They turned off the road into a path that led to a small group of unpainted buildings, resting on the white grassless earth, under enormous oaks. The path was almost a road, for there were ruts on each side where the Rabbit had been driven in and out, and perhaps a horse and cart.

Jenny thought she saw a horse in the barnyard ahead. They walked into the enclosure through the open gate between tall crepe myrtles. The loose fence which rambled about served merely to define the Harrison homestead, not to keep anything out or in. Nearer to the barn Jenny saw another stouter fence which kept the animals in the barnyard.

"It's a nice place," said Jenny.

The buildings were grouped charmingly about the space, and paths meandered from house to barn to shed. There was a roofed shelter near the gate with huge iron pots, big as witches' cauldrons, hung over a brick stove.

"That's where they boil the syrup," said Aunt Linda, "and over there is where the mule is hitched to grind the cane. Oh, I wish I could bring you out for the sugar cane grinding — that is lots of fun. Not many people grind cane any more. It's all done in factories nowadays."

They looked at the millstones and the long arm by which the stones were turned and imagined the mule moving around.

Brown hens roamed at will everywhere. A coat of whitewash, which had been given some buildings at Jenny's right, was a dull glow of faint white against the dark green of piney woods and palmettos. Not far away the woods merged into a jungle swamp where dead cypresses, gray as the house, stood deep in dark water.

"I declare, I'm afraid they are not home," said Aunt Linda in a tone slow with disappointment. She sank down on the steps of the porch and put

Lovable beside her, easing her arms by moving her shoulders.

The curtains were drawn. The doors were tight.

"Shall I knock anyway?" asked Jenny.

Aunt Linda said "Yes," but they all knew it was no use.

Lovable, catching the mood, wrinkled up his face. Jenny sat down. It was Cora who knocked, and then went and tried to peek under the curtain. Harry was chasing the chickens. "Shoo, shoo," he said.

There was a big bush of four o'clocks beside the steps. Jenny began to thread them together on a stem to make a chain. It was nice here — really nicer than having to talk to strange people, even the Harrisons. When she had finished her chain she would go and look at the animals.

Lovable leaned against his mother and fell asleep. She lifted him and put him in the cart, tilting it back so that he could lie almost flat. Then she came back and sat beside Jenny.

"I love the country," said Aunt Linda, and sat there with her hands in her lap, gazing at it all.

Jenny finished the flower chain and laid it on her aunt's dress. Then she went to see the Leghorns which had been gathered into the coop by Mr. Harrison before he left.

*　　*　　*

When it became certain that Mr. Harrison would not be back with the Rabbit in time to take them to the bus, they set out on foot. The sun was going down in a hot blaze behind the woods.

"That's a strange sky," said Aunt Linda. "Troubled weather, looks like." Jenny saw the long lines of a wind cloud like a horse's tail blowing across the sky. " 'Mackerel skies and mares' tails make lofty ships take in their sails,' " quoted Aunt Linda.

Jenny had to carry the baby's cart over most of the way back. The white sand and the deep ruts of the road made walking difficult, but Jenny ploughed through it stoutly, and the twins trailed behind.

"We must try to keep together," said Aunt Linda as the shadows began to gather. The sky was blotted out and the air grew chilly. A little wind sprang up to worry them.

"How far is it?" asked Jenny, humping and bumping and dragging the baby's cart.

"Not far now," said Aunt Linda, trying to sound cheerful. "Does anyone feel like singing with me? How about 'Swing low, sweet chariot, comin' for to carry me home'?" She began to sing.

They were so tired. The heavy sand slowed them up, and where there were pine needles they seemed to cut the soles of their feet that began to feel tender and sore.

The cart became an adversary to Jenny. It seemed to stick in the sand, or catch on the roots alongside on purpose. It hit her shins. She moved like a sleepwalker. She could not watch where she was going, for she no longer cared.

" 'What did I see-ee, comin' for to carry me home?' " sang Aunt Linda. "Sing, Harry, don't lag behind. 'Swing low, sweet chariot, comin' for to carry me...' "

"*I'm* carrying the chariot," Jenny said, and they all laughed.

"Not much further — just a step," said Aunt Linda. "We must be brisk. We can't afford to miss the bus. It will soon be black dark."

Oh, the agony of going forward. It seemed to Jenny that they had been walking for hours.

Suddenly Aunt Linda stood still and held out her hand. "Could that be rain?"

"Just drizzle," said Jenny.

Cora Belle began to whimper. "I'm tired, Mama, and I'm getting cold."

"I know, dear, be brave. There's the clearing just ahead."

Jenny looked at Aunt Linda's tired face, and she thought that when she grew up she would make things better for her.

"Let's race with Hildegarde," cried Jenny, making a desperate effort, for there were lights ahead. The bus must be in. They mustn't miss it!

"I think the bus is here," cried Aunt Linda at the same moment and tried to run with Lovable in her arms. She couldn't do it after that long walk. "Run ahead, Jenny, and ask him to wait," panted Aunt Linda.

Jenny went careening through the woods, across the pine needles, through the palmettos which leaned out to scratch her legs sharply, the cart clattering behind her, the twins after her. "Don't let Hildegarde win, Harry," called Jenny to spur him on. "There's a prize for this race. It comes from the ash-cans."

She heard the whirring sound of the motor beating through the quiet. The door clanged shut. She shouted to the motorman: "Wait! Oh, please wait!" but either he did not hear, or he did not care, for the big bus turned in its tracks and gathering speed went out of the woods, just as they reached the spot where they should have boarded it and Aunt Linda only a few paces behind them. Jenny thought her heart would burst.

The rain was falling more steadily now and it was dark there at the edge of the woods. The twins began to howl at exactly the same time in the same voice. Lovable joined his indignant wail to theirs. The rain came down even faster.

"Oh, no!" cried Aunt Linda to heaven, but it didn't stop the rain.

Jenny added tears to the rain on her cheeks. She felt angry. Her heart was still pounding fiercely.

"That was a mean man," said Harry.

Aunt Linda tried to laugh. "I reckon one can learn patience standing in the rain as well as anywhere else."

Jenny was glad Aunt Linda said that. She had forgotten to remember not to be angry. Aunt Linda was so wise. Jenny moved closer to her. She didn't think any more about the driver of the bus.

They huddled helplessly together under the downpour. It became one of those slashing summer storms that so thoroughly soak the dry earth in a brief time. Their thin clothing was soon dripping. They were cold. The clouds had closed over the sky and all light was withdrawn from them. Lovable cried bleakly.

Aunt Linda put Lovable into his cart. The baby did not find the clammy fabric a fair exchange for his mother's arms, and began to scream.

"My arms ache," said Aunt Linda to no one in particular. She patted Lovable and tried to sing a song about Noah and the rain, but had to give it up. The trees tossed and creaked in the wind. It was dark and frightening there at the edge of the woods. The macadam road ended a few yards away and the place they stood in was where the bus turned around and picked up any passengers who might be waiting at the end of the line.

"Would we be better off near the road?" asked Jenny.

"I was wondering myself," replied Aunt Linda, "but he might not stop for us there."

"It was just a suggestion of Hildegarde's," said Jenny.

"Who?" asked Aunt Linda, and the twins giggled.

"The birds will make you raincoats of pine needles," said Hildegarde, "so this won't happen again."

"Are you talking through your nose?" asked Aunt Linda.

"Why don't *you* have a raincoat of pine needles?" demanded the practical Cora.

"Because I can whistle for my fireflies," said

Jenny. "The ones that light my house for me, and they come swarming and make a sort of umbrella over my head, and the light is so strong that any rain that does fall is hot, so if you like, I could make you a cup of tea."

They all laughed because it sounded so ridiculous.

"Jenny, you are really absurd!" said Aunt Linda.

"Buy me a raincoat, Mama!" exclaimed Harry.

"Some day," answered his mother patiently. "Some day I certainly shall."

"When our ship comes in?"

"When our ship comes in," she agreed.

Jenny took Lovable's bottle from the pocket of the cart. "Do you think Lovable's bottle is too cold, Aunt Linda?"

"No, give it to him. I'll have to risk it," she answered.

With Lovable quieted, Jenny remarked suddenly, "I hope the elephants won't mind our being so wet."

"What elephants?" asked Aunt Linda.

Jenny used Hildegarde's voice, but in a rather guarded way, so as not to arouse Aunt Linda.

"I have sent some elephants to pick you up. They are wearing red and gold blankets, so you will be dry in a jiffy. Cora and Harry may keep them when they get home, for someone has just made me a present of seven cream-colored horses with black manes and hooves...." Jenny had read about the seven horses in some book and had pigeonholed it for future use. "I'd lend you the horses, but in this rain the paint might come off their hooves."

"I don't know what you're talking about, Jenny. Must you be so foolish?"

"Oh, Mama, can we keep the elephants?"

"Now you see what you've started," said Aunt Linda sternly. "You'll have to tell them there aren't any elephants."

"Oh, but there are! In India, in Africa, and so how can we tell about Florida? You might meet an elephant on any lonely road...especially if you see a lot of ash-cans."

The twins laughed and laughed. They knew something that their mother didn't.

"In fact, I think that may be the elephants now," said Jenny, as the glaring headlights of the bus appeared in the distance. They huddled together. The headlights lit the heavy slanting lines of rain as it swung around. Oh, how glad they were to see it! How warm and dry it seemed!

"Sorry to get your nice bus all wet," Aunt Linda said to the bus driver.

The lights were so bright after the dark lonesome woods that they blinked and squinted as they went to their seats. Their clothes dried out quickly as soon as they were inside.

"Why is it so hard to have a simple little day in the country," asked Aunt Linda, holding the sleeping baby so that his eyes were shaded from the light. "And why does it always seem to rain? That's to make it interesting, I suppose."

They slept. Such a heavy weary sleep all the way home. And when they got to their corner, how hard Harry fought not to get off, hitting out at Jenny, who tried to help him.

"Come on, son," urged the bus driver.

The children stumbled those last blocks over the concrete pavements in misery. Jenny thought that every bone in her body was aching. She must remember to ask Dr. Oliver how many bones she had. They did not even know when they arrived home, or how they tumbled into bed. They had been asleep from the time they got on the bus.

When Jenny woke up the next morning she was surprised to find herself in her nightdress. "Did you undress me?" she asked Aunt Linda.

"I helped," her aunt answered, smiling.

"I don't remember a single thing about it," said Jenny.

Mystery

Whenever she went to see Sam, Jenny would stop
by the greenhouses. She loved the long curious-
sounding names of the plants. She said them to
herself bouncing along the streets. She made up
tunes for them as she swept the kitchen floor.

> Bergamot when it's hot,
> Sage and basil when it's not.
> Hyssop
> For a bishop.
> Parsley green and neat,
> Leaves are good to eat.
> Mint to use in tea.
> Rue for you and me,
> Dill for Cora Bill,

Dell for Cora Belle...
Dill, dell, dill, dell...
Jenny rang a little bell merrily in her throat.
Angelica for Linda,
And thyme for us all!
Then she thought of something else:
Florida has an orchid
with a funny pod.
We get vanilla from it...
Praise God.
Jenny skipped happily and murmured, "Praise God, praise God!"

She enjoyed astonishing Dr. Oliver by her quick memory. When she saw that it amused him she worked hard, now and then even adding an easy Latin word to her store of knowledge, for she wanted to do something that would show him how grateful she was for what he had done for Sam.

Dr. Oliver talked to her about the characteristics of the flower families, and explained a few things about the structure of leaves. One day he spread out her hand, palm down.

"See how the veins of your hands run into the fingers," he said. "Leaves have veins, too." He gave her a big leaf and showed her the thick arteries. "When we get outside we'll hold it up to the sunlight and see the network of little veins running to the edges."

"I'm glad you can't just pick my hand off like a leaf," Jenny remarked, "because I wouldn't know how to grow another."

When Robert wasn't too busy he would explain the purpose of some experiment they were making, or tell her amazing stories of how soy beans were made into automobiles, or milk into winter coats. The world around her was proving to be much more wonderful than the tales in the green book.

Jenny told Robert about her new friend and the invitation to the theatre. Robert was surprised and seemed very much interested.

"So Miss Clare's back," he said. "I'd like mighty well to see her." He stirred up the soil around the roots of a small bush he was transplanting, his face thoughtful.

"Shall I ask her over to look at the greenhouses?"

He smiled. "By all means, but I don't think she'd come."

"Why not?"

"You'll know soon enough. It's not my place to tell you." Robert put peat moss into the loose earth.

Jenny was puzzled. What could be the reason? Perhaps Miss Clare had been a friend of Dr. Oliver's wife. That might be it.

"Was Dr. Oliver's wife beautiful?" she asked, hoping to find out.

"Very, very beautiful, and very, very nice. You've seen her."

"I've seen her! When? Oh, tell me, please!"

"I've told you now," said Robert.

Jenny persisted. "Do I know her to speak to? You don't mean Miss Clare, do you? But you said she was far away."

"So she was, when I said that." Robert went into the greenhouse.

Then Jenny knew...she was almost sure...for if he had not meant Miss Clare, who else could he possibly mean?

It was Maisie who told her what she really wanted to know.

Maisie saw her skipping by and called her in to have a slice of the chocolate cake she had just baked.

Jenny sat in the garden enjoying it and drinking a glass of milk.

"Miss Clare told me to keep an eye out for you," said Maisie. "She wanted you to be sure not to forget tomorrow. She has the tickets."

"I couldn't forget a thing like that," said Jenny. She looked happily around. "I love this place!"

"It is nice, but the big house was better."

"What big house?"

"Where Miss Clare lived before...the big stone house."

"Was Miss Clare...did Miss Clare...is Miss Clare...?" Jenny stammered, and still was unable to ask.

"Is she Mrs. King? Yes, she is. You didn't know? Everybody else knows. She's separated from him, but don't let on to her that I've been talking."

"Doesn't she love him any more?" asked Jenny fearfully.

"She loves him, all right. She never thinks of anything else."

"Then *why*...?" asked Jenny.

"You're asking *me?*" Maisie said in return.

The next morning Jenny told the twins in secrecy about her invitation to the theatre for that afternoon. Cora agreed to clean up if there was any trouble with Aunt Linda. Meals were irregular in that household, so it was possible that they might be having "something to eat" at the very moment that Jenny must start out with Miss Clare. But everything turned out very well.

Aunt Linda, taking Lovable with her, went out to see a customer, return some work, and collect a bill. Although other sewing had come in, meanwhile, it was the same customer, the same work, the same bill.

With her aunt away, Jenny was free to take a bath and get ready to go out without having to submit to questions. She had hidden her clothes in the woodshed. She finished her bath and put on her underwear, shivering, for there was only cold water running in the bathtub. When anyone wanted a hot bath in that house, water had to be heated in kettles and pots on the kerosene stove, but today Jenny would have bathed in the Arctic.

She wrapped a towel around her and scurried across the yard to the shed. It was safer that way. Aunt Linda was quick about everything; she might return any minute.

Jenny put on the red and white polka dot that was her only good dress, and around her waist she tied Cora's blue sash. She decided to let her hair flow loose and tie a ribbon around it, a fashion she had seen on some of the girls in Clearhope. She unbraided her hair and combed out the long strands. She had borrowed her aunt's high-heeled shoes and put them on her bare feet. She knew the shoes would never be missed, for her aunt seldom wore them. The shoes were big for Jenny, but fortunately they had a strap around the ankle which helped to hold them on.

"I don't like my toes sticking out of these shoes," said Jenny. "I'm just going to have to borrow a pair of your mother's stockings, Cora Belle. Please go and get them for me. I need something to fill in, so's I can keep them on."

Cora went, eager to be part of the adventure.

"I'm not satisfied with this blue sash," said Jenny, pulling it about. "Go see if you can find me something red, Harry."

"What kind of something?"

"Oh, like a ribbon or a strip of cloth, and bring something red I can tie my hair back with. Please hurry. Look in the scrap bag. I need something about this long." She measured the air with nervous hands.

Cora came back with the stockings just as Harry went into the house.

Jenny put them on but she could not keep them up. They felt smooth and yet strange on her sunburned legs.

"Harry has some rubber bands on his slingshot." Cora ran to get them. They were heavy broad bands but they were tight even on Jenny's small knees, yet they would have to do.

"I hope they won't squeeze me to death," she muttered.

Harry brought a piece of red cotton cloth. It was a triangular length left from some work of Aunt Linda's. Jenny turned it over. It had little to recommend it except its color, but if she twisted it into a roll she could tie her hair back with it. "I'll be late!" she murmured, knotting the cotton strip hastily on her head.

Jenny did not own a hat, but Cora had insisted that she wear her aunt's, and Cora herself had taken it from its box and its nest of tissue paper, and hidden it behind the woodpile wrapped in a clean kitchen towel. Jenny put it on. She turned around slowly before the twins.

"I'm ready. How do I look?"

"Fine," said Harry.

"You look grown-up," said Cora Belle.

Jenny kept giving little twitches to her costume. "Cora, are you *sure* I look all right?" she asked hoarsely. Something seemed to have gone wrong with her voice. "You're sure I don't look just awful?"

"You look pretty."

"If I can only keep these shoes on. And the hat! It's mighty big, too!"

Jenny started off, but she had only reached the sidewalk when she met Aunt Linda hurrying home pushing Lovable in his cart. She stood stricken, wondering what to do. Aunt Linda gave a little scream. For a minute she looked as though she couldn't even be sure that it was Jenny.

"What on earth!" she exclaimed. "What have you dressed yourself up for...like a plush horse? Come inside this instant and take off those things. That's my only pair of nylons and not intended for a game."

"It's not a game, Aunt Linda. I'm invited...I'm invited to go to the theatre. Please don't stop me." Her voice failed, she could only whisper the last words.

"She's going to a theatre," cried the twins in chorus.

Aunt Linda stood stern and uncomprehending.

"Oh, Aunt Linda, that lady...you know...I found her dog, and she rewarded me? She asked me if I'd like to go to the theatre...and it's happening right now! She's waiting for me...so please may I go, Aunt Linda?"

"Seems to me you're a little late in asking me if you can go," said her aunt. "You can't go like that, that's the first thing."

"You don't want me to wear your hat?"

"That's the least of it." She put her hand to her

forehead. "Let me think what to do."

"I'll be careful of your things, Aunt Linda."

"Jenny, they don't matter. It's you that matters. You mustn't go off in clothes twenty years too old for you. Come inside and let's see what I can do."

"I'll be late! I'll be late!" wailed Jenny. "Oh, please, let me wear them just this once. Oh, please, Aunt Linda!" She began to jiggle up and down and her face was all screwed up.

"Jenny, control yourself. Everything will be all right." Aunt Linda put a hand on her shoulder and turned her toward the house. "Cora Belle, bring the baby," she called.

Jenny looked at her uncertainly but was reassured when Aunt Linda smiled and said, "Isn't it wonderful that you are invited to go to the theatre?"

"You don't mind?"

"I am delighted. Why wouldn't I be glad when something so nice happens to someone I love!"

She guided Jenny to the mirror and faced her towards it. "Now, let's see. You know, Jenny, they say the well-dressed woman looks in the mirror before she goes out to see what she has put on that she can do without. Take off the hat."

Jenny was reluctant. "I think the hat looks

fine, Aunt Linda." She slanted her eyes up from under the brim, holding her head as straight as possible so that it wouldn't slip off.

Aunt Linda held out her hand. Jenny gave her the hat.

"Now the shoes and stockings. Goodness, what have you on your knees? They're enough to stop the circulation."

"They're mine!" said Harry, reclaiming the rubber bands.

"Your dress looks fresh and pretty," went on Aunt Linda, "but I think it needs a red belt. I'll make you one in no time, while you braid your hair. Don't go with your hair flying like that, it isn't suitable."

"I like it this way," Jenny said stubbornly.

"Be a good girl and braid it up. She invited a little girl with braids to go to the theatre, and that's the one she wants to take with her."

Jenny was unconvinced.

"Be your honest self," said Aunt Linda, "there's nothing better." She had found a piece of material and was stitch-stitching and cross-stitching a belt for Jenny.

Jenny brushed and braided her hair. "What time is it? I'm going to miss everything."

"No, you won't. When you do right, it comes

out right. Jenny, I believe I have a piece of red silk ribbon somewhere that would be enough to make two bows for your hair." Aunt Linda searched in her sewing box, found the ribbon, cut it in two. "Let me tie it for you," she said, putting bows on the pigtails. Then she fastened the belt on her.

"You look sweet," Aunt Linda told her. "Believe me, you do. Now hurry off and have a good time."

"But my feet, Aunt Linda," Jenny exclaimed. "You know I can't go to a party without shoes!"

"Dear child, what can we do? You haven't any."

"You could let me wear yours."

"Now, Jenny, they have high heels and they are too big for you. Don't you think it's silly to go swimming in gunboats up the aisle of a theatre?"

"I need some shoes." Jenny's underlip trembled.

"Well, try these low heels I have on." Aunt Linda slipped out of the sandals she was wearing and Jenny stepped into them. Her thin feet were several sizes too small.

"They are bigger than the others," she said, and she began to cry.

"Don't cry!" consoled Aunt Linda. "You'll

have a red nose for the party. And it won't change anything." She put her arms around Jenny.

"Jenny, this is the hardest lesson to learn: to be brave when you are humiliated. It *isn't* just right that you have to go in bare feet to the theatre, but the big thing is that you have a chance to go! Many children with shoes aren't going to be there. She didn't ask *them*. My mother told me there are two kinds of pride. One is false pride, and it makes you care about the wrong thing, makes you want to dress better than you can afford to, and pretend to be something you're not...the other makes you grateful for what comes and too proud to pretend. You must go, just as you are. You're a little girl. It doesn't make any difference, really."

"It makes a difference to me."

"Don't be ashamed of what you cannot help. Have a good time, anyway."

"I don't want to go. Can't Harry run and tell her I'm not coming?" Jenny sat down on the sofa, miserable.

Aunt Linda knelt down beside Jenny and held her arms around her. "Jenny, go for my sake. If you miss this, it will be because I haven't given you any shoes, so it is my fault. Don't you see that it is hard enough for me to bear that you haven't what you need, without making you miss a good time besides? Please go for me."

Jenny kept her head bent.

"Your mother would tell you to go if she were here," her aunt said.

"I'll go, Aunt Linda. Do I look all right...except for my feet?"

"You look just beautiful," said her aunt, kissing her. "You look just the way a little girl should look, and I'm telling you the truth."

Aunt Linda and the twins came to the front of the house to see her off. Jenny waved at them from the street. She walked slowly at first, and then she began to leap and run and skim along the pavements in her own particular way.

Jenny as an Angel

The theatre was red and gold. Jenny sat enraptured in a box, clutching the railing that separated her from the stage. It was covered with velvet. She slid her fingers back and forth, stroking it. Just below her hand was the curving wood of the stage, a few feet further was the mysterious golden curtain, softly lighted at the edges. She wanted to ask questions but she couldn't speak. It was enchanting, overwhelming. She trembled with excitement like a little colt when he finds his legs for the first time.

The house buzzed with subdued conversation. It was a wonderful sound. Bees, thought Jenny, great big giant bees.

The lights were going out. What was happening? Slowly but surely the lights were going out. Jenny glanced at Miss Clare and saw that she was calm. Then the light at the foot of the curtain brightened. The music began. The curtain was moving, was rising.

Music beat upon her, it seemed to be coming from her own heart. She followed the quick changes breathlessly. Fluttering dancers came together and were blown apart by the melody, their rainbow draperies floating like mist. Others began to talk, chatting in a strange language.

Jenny nudged Miss Clare. "They speaking French?" she asked in a whisper.

"English. Listen carefully. You'll understand."

Jenny fastened her eyes upon the stage, put her elbows on her knees and her chin in her hands. She did catch a word now and then.

There was more singing, and the pretty Iolanthe came very close to the box. She was talking to a tall man. Jenny stared. Who did the man make her think of? The ageless fairy and the men of her story danced and sang, approaching and then moving away from the side of the stage nearest Jenny. She leaned forward. Her memory was a bit hazy, but surely that man was her vanished Uncle Henry!

Jenny stood up to see better. There was a slight stir from the people just behind them, as Miss Clare with quick hands seized her and pulled her firmly back into her seat.

Jenny whispered, "That looks like my Uncle Henry."

"Stay right here," Miss Clare whispered back, holding on to her. "I'm sure it isn't. That man comes from *England.*"

The stage was full of people, of dazzle, of motion, of heavenly sound. There was a burst of music. The curtain fell. The audience applauded. The lights came on.

Iolanthe and the man Jenny had thought looked like Uncle Henry came out and bowed. His face was covered with a sort of mask of dough, and his eyes had black smeared on them. Jenny saw that it wasn't Uncle Henry at all.

"I made a mistake," she said apologetically, as they left the theatre when the play was over. "But if I ever meet him anywhere, I'll give him a piece of my mind. Aunt Linda says I take it too hard, that it's no use to look back."

"Perhaps she's right," said Miss Clare. "What did he do?"

"He just walked right out and left her without any money to take care of the children, and Lovable was on the way so she couldn't go out and get regular work." Jenny was indignant when she thought of it.

"How did she manage?" Miss Clare was sympathetic.

"Well, she said she couldn't just sit and mope. She had too much to do. She could sew real well, so she took in sewing. She just went up to the front door and asked if anybody who lived there wanted anything sewed."

"And did they?" Miss Clare wanted to know.

"Well, not very many," Jenny admitted. "Aunt Linda thinks it's because we don't live in the right place. If we lived on the other side of the river near Green Street, she thinks she'd sew for people who like fine work and have the money to pay for it."

"Do you suppose she would make something for me? I'll bring some material and a pattern."

Jenny laughed. "She doesn't need a pattern. You just tell her what you want and leave it to her."

"I'll be there to see her tomorrow." Then Miss Clare was silent, looking at the road ahead.

Jenny wondered what she was thinking about. Dr. Oliver, maybe? What had happened to separate these two people who seemed to Jenny more fascinating than any she had found in the pages of books? Perhaps Miss Clare wasn't a queen, but she looked like one, so proud and straight and lovely. What had she done to Dr. Oliver, or he to her? Was she like the pitiless beauty in the fairy tales? Did the princess have dark sad eyes and smooth shining hair? When she smiled did it light all the air the way Miss Clare did?

"You must tell me how your dog is getting on?" Miss Clare spoke suddenly.

"He's getting better. Dr. Oliver may take the splints off today. I'm going by there before I go home."

"I'll drop you off," said Miss Clare.

"I'm learning all about the plants in the greenhouses," Jenny confided. "I had no idea there were so many different kinds."

Miss Clare smiled at her.

"I wish I could do something for Dr. Oliver, he's so good," said Jenny.

Miss Clare said nothing.

"But he says he only wants the moon or the morning star and they are far away!"

"Not so far," replied Miss Clare. "The moon is tied to the earth. It's a law. I'm surprised he doesn't know that."

Jenny remembered that Aunt Linda had once

said that some people belong together, and that they can't get away from each other no matter how hard they try. She wanted to say that now, but she didn't know how. Besides there was something else that she wanted to talk about.

"Miss Clare," she asked, "when you were traveling did you ever see snow?"

Miss Clare told her about the Alps, and how she had gone skiing there, and of how snow felt on your face. And she described the snow-covered mountains towering all around.

Jenny had read about other places and she asked Miss Clare about them, too, and Miss Clare told her stories of strange people and fascinating things she had seen.

Jenny's eyes were like stars as she listened.

They turned into the big gates and Miss Clare drove her to the side entrance.

"Thank you for everything," said Jenny. "It was a wonderful party."

"I enjoyed it, too," said Miss Clare. "We will have another soon. Be sure and tell your aunt that I'll come tomorrow."

Jenny was out of the car now. Oh, if only she could bring Miss Clare to Dr. Oliver!

"Wouldn't you like to see Sam?" she suggested, coming back and looking in the car window.

"Yes, bring him to see me when he's well," said Miss Clare. Yet she, too, seemed to be lingering as though there was something on her mind that urged her to stay, that held her, almost against her will. "I'll wait for you, if you are not too long," she said finally. "I'll take you home. It's getting quite dark."

"I'm not afraid... but that would be lovely," Jenny added hastily.

She raced towards the house. Should she tell Dr. Oliver that Miss Clare was there? But how would that change anything, for after all Miss Clare lived just down the street and they never saw each other!

Jenny stumbled and fell sprawling on the stone steps. Another skinned knee, she thought cheerfully. Then she saw Miss Clare spring out of the car and run towards her.

"Ooooh! Help me, Dr. Oliver!" cried Jenny, not moving. There was no sound in the house, but the light from the study streamed into the darkness.

"Dr. Oliver! Dr. Oliver!" cried Jenny again, loudly. "Help me, *please!*" Miss Clare was bending over her anxiously.

"Oh! Have you twisted your ankle, Jenny? Are you all right?"

"I think so," Jenny answered truthfully. "No. Yes. I mean I haven't twisted it. It's only my knee." But she didn't move. *Where* was Dr. Oliver? Miss Clare was pulling on her elbow, trying to help her up, as Dr. Oliver came quickly across the terrace.

"Jenny, are you hurt?" he called.

"No, I'm all right." She sat up. She began to feel ashamed and embarrassed. Their concern was so real. The scratched place on her knee was bleeding. She was glad of that. She wished that she had something more to show. "I'm sorry I scared you," she said.

Miss Clare's hand fell from Jenny's arm as Dr. Oliver came closer.

"Why, Clare!" he said.

"Hello, Oliver."

They didn't say anything more, but stood staring at each other, forgetting Jenny, but she felt that the air was crackling all around her. Jenny wanted to scramble up and run away, but she said instead, "Will you help me up, please?" She put up her hand.

"She may have sprained her ankle," said Miss Clare. "We had better get her inside."

"Lean on me, Jenny," said Dr. Oliver.

Jenny seized Miss Clare's hand and clung to it. She limped a little. It seemed only polite, they were so kind to her. She thought to herself that if she got through this, she'd never pretend again.

"Does your foot hurt?" asked Dr. Oliver, putting her into a chair. He knelt down and felt the bones in her foot and ankle with his wonderful healing fingers. Miss Clare looked on with a solicitous face.

"Nothing broken there," said Dr. Oliver.

"I feel fine. I'm all right. Just my knee," said Jenny, eager to be finished with it.

Dr. Oliver touched the knee swiftly, rocked it back and forth. "Just a scratch," he said cheerfully. He sounded relieved. "I'll put a bandage on." He stuck a band-aid over the skinned place.

"I'll wait in the car for you, Jenny," said Miss Clare. "We've been to the theatre together," she explained, feeling his eyes on her.

But he said nothing. He just looked at her.

"You seem well," said Miss Clare.

"So do you. You look wonderful. A little thin perhaps. You are not taking your vitamins."

"No, I'm not."

"Did you have a good time?"

"Oh, yes, it was a lovely trip. I don't know why I came back, really."

"What did you do?"

"Oh...oh...heavens...everything! Sightseeing, of course, met some interesting people. Saw the Coliseum...theatres were nice in London ...marvelous in fact...Paris..." She did not meet his eyes.

"Well, it would be nice to have nothing to do but dash around the world for over half a year...but I couldn't leave my work."

"Of course, that must come first," said Miss Clare in a cool voice. "I suppose it still takes all your time...you stay up all night...wear yourself out."

"Now, Clare, you're the one that's all worn out. You're much too thin! I'm going to give you some vitamins, and I hope you'll take them." He took a bottle from the drawer of the desk.

"No, thank you," she said, so angrily that Jenny was startled. "We meet quite by accident, and I find I am still a guinea pig!"

"Oh?" he seemed angry, too. "If that's the way you interpret honest concern, I'm sorry. I see you pale and thin. I'm a doctor. I'd do the same for any waif or stray cat on the path."

"Well, *thank* you again!"

"I can't imagine what has upset you!"

Jenny couldn't imagine either.

"Oh, you've forgotten perhaps that you tried out the *nettle juice* on me...for low blood count. And seaweed sprinkled on my cereal every morning. I've forgotten what *that* was for."

"Iodine," he answered. "But, Clare dear..."

"Oh, iodine!" she repeated bitterly. "And for Christmas you gave me that horrible perfume that you made from a root. You said it would be different when it came out of the bottle!" The tears were rolling down her cheeks and she shook the words out between sobs. "So thank you very much, I think I'll just be myself no matter how unattractive."

Dr. Oliver looked at his wife in astonishment. "You're crying!" he exclaimed. "Why? Clare, Clare darling! Don't! I wouldn't hurt you again for all the world." He put his arms around her. "What is the matter? I'll never understand you."

She fumbled for her handkerchief, weeping like a child. "Oh, it's just that here we go, saying the same old things." She buried her face against him.

"I thought once that we were like Juliet and Romeo...Francesca and what's his name," she sobbed.

"How do you know we're not?" he asked, and he bent and kissed her.

After a minute Miss Clare said, "I don't care if your work *is* more important, Oliver."

"But, darling, it isn't! Listen, Clare, it isn't. Nothing matters but you, and that we should be together."

Jenny was crying because Miss Clare was crying. It was awful to have them so miserable. She thought she had better go away, since they had forgotten her, but Miss Clare heard her as she went to the door.

"Oh, Jenny, wait." A moment before she had been crying, but now she turned in Dr. Oliver's arms and smiled dazzlingly. Jenny stared in amazement.

"You're not crying, Jenny? Why, you should be glad because we are happy."

"You're happy?" questioned Jenny. It was a little puzzling.

"Yes," said Dr. Oliver, "and we owe it all to you. I've got my wife back, and I'm never going to let her go again."

"Jenny, you were our good angel," said Miss Clare.

Jenny was pleased at the praise, but she didn't know what to say.

"How is Sam today?" asked Jenny.

She wondered why they laughed. Dr. Oliver immediately led them into the next room where Sam was frisking and leaping in his box.

"We'll soon have him out again," said Dr. Oliver, "though I am still a bit doubtful about the strength of that leg."

When they had petted and praised Sam, Miss Clare thought that it was time to take Jenny home, and Dr. Oliver said that he would drive, so that he could be sure that his wife would find her way back to the place where she really lived. "She may have forgotten where she belongs," he said to Jenny.

Jenny sat on the front seat between them. She was deep in a daydream.

How wonderful it would be, she thought, if Dr. Oliver and Miss Clare would ask her to come and live in the big house with them.

"You'd be my very own daughter," she imagined him saying. "You should have a father." But of course she couldn't do it. She would have to disappoint him.

"I couldn't leave Aunt Linda," she would say. "She depends on me. She couldn't get along without me. But thank you very much," said Jenny to the tall sad figure of Dr. Oliver in her mind. This time he *was* wearing a crown.

It was a moonless night. Jenny could hardly see a thing as they let her out in front of her house, but she knew the way. She ran quickly through the blackness.

"Good-bye," she called to them.

"Good-bye, good-bye!"

"Good-bye, *darling!*" answered Miss Clare.

The Ship Comes In

The day that Miss Clare came to see Aunt Linda
was a most important day. When Jenny thought
about it afterwards, it seemed to her that all the
wonderful things that followed began to take
shape on that day.

The change had begun when she met Dr.
Oliver. She knew that he was her friend and that
Miss Clare was, too. She had told Dr. Oliver
things that she would never tell another living
soul, not even Sam. She thought perhaps her father might have been like Dr. Oliver, only she
couldn't remember her father. It was a wonderful
feeling to have friends.

Jenny saw Miss Clare getting out of her car,

and climbed down from the oak tree to meet her. She swung down the last few feet on the stout old vine that twined among the branches and over the fence.

Jenny took Miss Clare inside. "This is my Aunt Linda," she said proudly.

Aunt Linda stopped the sewing machine when they came into the room. "Gracious, I'm afraid everything is upside down," she said. She sprang up and smiled in a pleased way, her head tilted so that the smile seemed to shine through her eyes. The sun fell on her hair and tipped her eyelashes with brightness.

The dress she was working on was spread out on sofa and table. She moved a chiffon skirt from the back of a chair.

"Won't you sit here?" she asked Miss Clare. "I promised Mrs. Mason I'd get this done for her to wear this weekend."

"Oh, how charming!" said Miss Clare. "I'm sorry to interrupt your work, but since Jenny and I have become such friends, I did want to meet you, and the baby, and see the twins again. Where is the baby?"

"He's asleep on the porch. He just loves to sleep to the sound of the sewing machine." Her eyes twinkled at the visitor.

Happiness had come into the room with Miss Clare. She looked as though she had been dipped in light. Everything about her sparkled: her pretty summer clothes, her bright shoes and hat were all part of a change in her. Even her voice was different, Jenny thought.

"I'll go bring Harry and Cora Bell," said Jenny, but she didn't go.

"Have you time to make a dress for me?" asked Miss Clare, giving Aunt Linda the material. "Jenny says that you don't need a pattern."

Aunt Linda spread the material upon the air, like a caravan merchant with a treasure from Cathay. The silk came to rest in billows over the machine.

"No, I don't use patterns." Her eyes were on Miss Clare, measuring, deciding. "This would be suitable for a full skirt that moves when you walk. I'd like it very simple and a neckline like this." Her skillful hands made a swift outline. "I'll make you an extra scarf. Shall I draw it for you?"

"No, I'll leave it to you." said Miss Clare, delighted.

While Aunt Linda was taking Miss Clare's measurements, Jenny ran to find the twins.

When they came in, Aunt Linda was holding the tape measure against Miss Clare's arm, so she only flapped stiff fingers at them. When Aunt Linda had written down the last inches, Miss Clare hugged Cora and patted Harry's shoulder. "If you like I'll take you for a little ride when I go," she offered. "Could you spare the twins for twenty minutes?" she asked.

"I can spare them for more than that," said Aunt Linda.

Harry knelt on the floor almost at Miss Clare's feet. He put his eye to a small hole in the linoleum. His sober close-cropped head almost touched the floor, and the rest of him rose in a hump towards the visitor. "What is it, Harry?" asked his mother, seeing Miss Clare's astonished look.

Harry sat back on his heels and smiled serenely at her. He waved his hand with a lordly gesture as though brushing away the whole matter. He had seen nothing in the hole in the floor, although it had looked inviting. "It is of no consequence," said Harry's gesture.

"I hope that I'll see you again soon, and my husband is anxious to meet you, too," said Miss Clare when she left, taking the twins and Jenny for the promised ride.

It was extraordinary how quickly Aunt Linda and Miss Clare became friends, and how much they had to talk about. Aunt Linda went to Miss

Clare's little house and brought back an armful of dresses to work on. One to be let down, a jacket to be pinched in, another to be changed to the style of a dress Miss Clare had brought home from Paris. She told Aunt Linda all about the fashions there, and showed her other things: a suit from London, sport clothes from Italy.

"You are welcome to copy anything I have," said Miss Clare. "I would have bought more, but clothes are terribly expensive in Europe."

There was so much for Aunt Linda to do that after a few days it was thought simpler for Aunt Linda to work in Miss Clare's house on Green Street which looked out over the garden, and from which she could see the children playing just below. The room had a very large table to cut on, and was lined with cupboards and shelves. It had, besides, an electric sewing machine.

"This will spoil me," said Aunt Linda happily. "Your house is just about perfect."

"I think it *is* perfect," said Jenny.

Miss Clare stopped in every day to talk to Aunt Linda, or to try on a dress, and when she took her books and music and clothes over to the big King place that week, she asked Aunt Linda to help her.

All the children went along to Miss Clare's house and played in the garden while the grown-ups rode back and forth in the car carrying boxes and suitcases and coats.

Maisie bustled about in a crisp blue dress, helping with the packing. She was kind and friendly to the children, and made a big fuss over Lovable.

"I declare that baby is the best child I *ever* saw," she exclaimed. "Just no trouble at all!"

Jenny did not agree but she was willing to leave it at that. She had promised Dr. Oliver that she would try to draw the leaves of the trees and bushes she saw, and so she was happy to have the children under Maisie's supervising eye while she wandered off with the notebooks and crayons that he had given her.

At noon Maisie called her. She was not trying to draw at that moment. She had discovered figs on the tree with the beautiful broad leaves at the edge of the lawn.

"May I eat a fig, Maisie?" she asked.

"Of course. Miss Clare said that you should just help yourself to anything you wish for," answered Maisie cheerfully. Maisie was always cheerful. "Come around to the back, I'll give you some lunch."

Jenny broke open a small green fig and swallowed the bright red center in two gulps. It was sweeter than honey. She snatched two more for the twins, and ran around the house. Maisie was spreading a gaily colored linen cloth over a table beside a persimmon tree.

"I'll give you a picnic here," said Maisie.

"What is a picnic?" asked Cora, biting into her fig.

"You don't *know*?" Maisie asked. "It's a party out-of-doors."

"I've read about them a lot," said Jenny to show that it was Cora Belle's youth which made her so ignorant.

While Maisie was putting the dishes on the table, Harry showed Jenny some strange low bushes he had found in the border.

"It's a shrimp plant," Jenny told them, examining the coral-pink overlapping flowers just the shape and color of a boiled shrimp. Robert had pointed out this plant to her only the day before. "It's real name is *Beloperone guttata*," said Jenny, bringing out the long words slowly.

"You're showing off!" cried Cora severely. She ran away with a disgusted air.

"I think you're just making it up," cried Harry, and he trotted off after Cora, for Maisie had come out of the house with something steaming in a big bowl.

Jenny stood for an instant, forlorn beside the

shrimp bushes. She had been so proud of learning the hard names of the flowers, and she had expected to be admired for it. A wave of disappointment swept over her. She ran after Cora.

"Please don't make me mad," begged Jenny. "I have a most awful feeling when you speak to me like that."

"I didn't mean anything," said Cora agreeably.

"Then it is quite all right," said Jenny, at peace again. "What is the name of this delicious thing I am eating?" she asked Maisie.

"That's a cheese souffle," answered Maisie, pleased. "I'm so glad you like it."

"Everything over here has a funny name, hasn't it?" remarked Harry. "May I have a little more of it, please?"

"You certainly may," replied Maisie, scraping the browned edges away from the glass dish. She divided what was left.

"But its real name is a picnic," said Cora.

"I feel mighty bad to take money for having so much fun," Aunt Linda said, when Miss Clare drove them home in the late afternoon.

"Nonsense," said Miss Clare. "What would I do without you? I am beginning to wonder how I ever got along before we met. Don't forget that you're having supper with us on Sunday."

On Sunday the weather was perfect.

"This is to celebrate my being back in my real home," said Miss Clare. "We are having supper on the terrace. Oliver and I have a marvelous idea we want to talk over with you."

Lovable slept in a big chair with cushions stuffed all around him, while the others were served sandwiches and hot chocolate, and salad from special plates.

"There is ice cream for dessert," Harry informed them.

"How do you know?" asked Dr. Oliver.

"I saw it in the kitchen. Peach. I like it best."

"I like it best, too," said Cora.

"Perhaps you would be willing to bring it out," suggested Dr. Oliver.

The twins ran around the side of the house.

Miss Clare was wearing the dress Aunt Linda had made for her. Dr. Oliver said it was that dress that convinced him Aunt Linda was a genius.

"Genius is a mighty big word," said Aunt Linda.

"We are sure that if you could hang out your shingle in a more convenient part of town, you'd have all the people to sew for that you could handle. It must be difficult to do your work in the house you are living in."

"It is," confessed Aunt Linda, "and the man who owns it won't fix it up, but to tell you the truth, it's the best I can do just now."

"Oh, Linda," exclaimed Miss Clare, her hands clasped and her eyes shining with eagerness, "I want to lend you my little house on Green Street."

Aunt Linda's eyes grew big. Jenny was afraid she might faint, she looked so white. She couldn't speak.

"We both want you to live in it," Miss Clare continued. "In a way we have come to think of Jenny as...well, almost as our own little girl. My husband especially."

"It's most kind of you, but it isn't possible," said Aunt Linda. "It's much too fine a house for us — I just couldn't manage it — I can hardly manage where we are!"

"Now, Linda, listen to me," insisted Miss Clare. "You'd have *no rent to pay*, and so you'd have all the money you make for food and clothes and incidentals. You'd have *less* expense than you have now. It's a very special house. I wouldn't like to have just anybody in it. There's that small room upstairs which you could keep for a sewing room. It has cupboards and a big table to cut out dresses on. Jenny will have a room to herself, and there is the garden for the children to play in. I

have a plan I thought we might work out in this way. If you do a day's sewing for me, say twice a month, and keep an eye on the place generally, we'd consider that the equivalent of rent. Oh, say you will!"

Aunt Linda looked from Miss Clare to Dr. Oliver. "It's almost too good to be true," she said, her voice shaking a little. "How could I refuse when you make it so easy?"

There was a breeze playing across the grass and tossing the branches so that they nodded up and down...yes, yes, yes! Everything was yes. Jenny was very happy. The sun dappled the terrace, moving with the shadows of the leaves as though the light were laid upon the wind.

Dr. Oliver patted Jenny's hand.

"Then it's settled," he said. "I'll get someone to help you move," he added to Aunt Linda.

"Don't forget that there is plenty of furniture already in the house," Miss Clare reminded him.

Harry and Cora Belle came out with the ice cream, followed by Maisie who carried a tray with plates and cakes. She served them and Dr. Oliver helped. Then he returned to the edge of the terrace where he had been sitting beside Jenny, and he gave her his cake.

"I have a book for you about flowers and their families," he said to her. "It is a very easy one and it has first-rate pictures in it. I think you'll find it useful."

"I know ever so many more names than last week," Jenny said.

"Good. Did you draw the outlines of the leaves?"

"Well, I tried," answered Jenny slowly.

"Try again. Keep at it. It's very important. When you start using a microscope, you'll have to draw a great deal."

"Don't let him rush you, Jenny. You don't really have to do that until you get to college." Miss Clare smiled.

"I'm not rushing her," said Dr. Oliver. "She has a gift for this, and a gift mustn't be slighted. There's no special age at which you take up the things that interest you. I believe that you should be helped when you want to begin."

"I love it," said Jenny. She was afraid for a moment that Miss Clare meant for her to give up learning about the plants.

"I have something for Jenny," said Dr. Oliver. Miss Clare smiled as though she knew what it was. Dr. Oliver let his hand rest lightly on her shoulder as he passed. Her eyes were full of understanding as she looked up at him, and she patted his hand before he took it away. He bent down and kissed the top of her head.

When he had gone into the house Miss Clare said, "When I was your age, Jenny, I was very interested in the stars. My mother gave me a book about astronomy, and that was a good excuse to stay up late. I remember I was worried for fear a gigantic meteor or comet would run into Earth, and knock it out of its orbit."

"I love music," said Aunt Linda.

"Do you sing, Linda?" asked Miss Clare. "Your voice is so soft and charming."

"No. I had music lessons as a child, though," answered Aunt Linda. "My father was very musical and he taught me."

"I was thinking," said Miss Clare, "that Jenny might enjoy studying music this winter."

Jenny wondered if she should say anything. She didn't know whether she wanted to take music lessons or not, winter seemed so far away. She moved over and stood beside her aunt's chair. Aunt Linda had a look of contentment on her face that Jenny had never seen there. The twins were finishing up a second helping of ice cream. They left the empty dishes on the edge of the terrace and ran off to play. Lovable slept on.

Dr. Oliver came back. In his arms was a small brown dog.

"Sam!" cried Jenny.

Dr. Oliver put him down.

On four strong legs Sam ran to Jenny. She picked him up in her arms. She could feel the tears on her cheeks.

"Oh, Dr. Oliver, I'm so happy!" she tried to say.

Sam, with a great burst of affection for all the world, wriggled from her grasp and rushed to wake up Lovable, jumping up on the chair and licking his face. Lovable opened his eyes in a drowsy way, stretching them wide under his lifted eyebrows. He gave a gentle cry, pulling his soft red mouth together in an O. Then Sam frisked down and flung himself upon Aunt Linda, lapping up her ice cream greedily, but for once Aunt Linda was not annoyed.

"Sam," she said, giving him a little hug, "at last we are going to have a house big enough for you to live in with us!"

"Oh, Aunt Linda, may he sleep at the foot of my bed in a basket?"

"I don't see why not," she said.

Having been petted by Miss Clare and Dr. Oliver, Sam came back and settled down beside Jenny. She put her arm around him.

In the distance the twins were playing in the garden. With exactly the same motions, and exactly the same earnest expression on each face, they were carrying the cut grass which lay in heaps on the lawn in imaginary buckets to feed imaginary animals. They seemed to be glued together side by side.

Aunt Linda and Jenny exchanged a smile at their twinishness.

Then suddenly they began to quarrel. The rhythm of their gestures was interrupted and Cora's voice was raised in excited argument.

Aunt Linda looked at Jenny. Neither of them wanted to have the peace of that wonderful day disturbed.

"Let me, Aunt Linda, I'll go," said Jenny, leaping to her feet to defend her family. She dashed down to them, Sam at her heels.

"Go on with your game," said Jenny. "It looked like fun."

"Harry keeps stepping where the cow is," said Cora.

"I've moved the cow," said Harry.

"I don't want her moved," said Cora Belle. "I've given in on everything today."

"What's her name?" asked Jenny.

"She didn't tell me."

"We'll ask Hildegarde to name her."

"Is Hildegarde coming?" Harry's eyes began to shine.

"I think so. There's a feeling in the air. Don't you feel it?"

"I do!" said Cora Belle.

A little breeze seemed to pass them by.

"Hildegarde does everything so fast. She stirs up the wind," said Jenny. "Hello, Hildegard!"

"Will you name our cow, Hildegarde?"

"What impertinence!" answered Hildegarde. "I wouldn't dream of it. You must wait until a name grows on her. But I'll *ask* her what her name may be." She stroked the imaginary nose and spoke to the cow. "That's pretty. That's really very pretty."

"What did she say? Tell us what her name is."

"Serena. Her name is Serena. Isn't that a cowish name? I believe I'll take her home with me. Do you give milk, Serena? We use just quantities in the ash-cans, so perhaps you'll have to work overtime." Hildegarde listened to the cow. "That's an idea. She says I could take both of them." She patted another head.

"Is there an extra cow there?" asked Harry in a surprised voice, staring at the empty space in front of Jenny.

"Certainly. Didn't you see her?" asked Hildegarde. "It's Bosky. Wait a minute, Bosky, wait a minute," she drawled cooingly. "Serena, where do you think you are going? No, Serena, you may not go up to the terrace and sit in the arm chair."

Cora Belle grabbed Jenny's dress. "Oh, let her go and sit in the arm chair, Jenny...I mean, Hildegarde. Think how surprised they'd be."

Jenny was tempted, but decided that it was better to keep the game in the garden. "No, I'll get them to the ash-cans before there is any trouble, but Serena, as soon as you get there, I'll put you in a big chair and serve you a cup of tea, with cream...if you'll very kindly supply cream." She waved her arms to send them off.

"Oh, Harry, you'll be interested," she called. "Bosky is the cow that gives condensed milk." She went off after them.

In a minute Jenny came back and dropped down on the grass beside a bush of hydrangea.

The twins watched her eagerly. Jenny rolled over on her elbows and spoke to something very small.

"What is it, Maudie?" she asked. *"It's Hildegarde's cook,"* she whispered to the twins. "Yes, Maudie? *Maudie is an otter.* On Fridays she catches the fish herself."

The twins sat down to listen.

"Hildegarde forgot something, but she has forgotten what she forgot." The twins thought this was funny.

"I know," said Maudie in a thin squeaky voice, "but I shan't tell her. Don't you tell her either, Cora."

"But I don't know," said Cora.

"Then *of course* you mustn't tell her!"

"Let's look about and see if we can find anything," suggested Jenny.

The twins searched the grass carefully and crawled under the evergreens.

"Isn't this her bag?" asked Jenny, picking up nothing gently from the grass heap.

"If it has a little nail brush and a white comb, and a powder puff," answered Maudie in a squeak.

Jenny looked. Cora and Harry peered into her cupped hands. Jenny nodded.

"Does she use a powder puff at her age?"

"No, she powders the guinea pigs after their bath," Maudie told them, then she said, "I'd like the recipe for ice cream soda, if you have it handy, and Hildegarde wants to be invited to your new house...but don't say I said so!"

"But of course we invite her. Don't we?"

"Yes, we do," said Cora Belle.

"Hildegarde knows how to make ice cream soda, with peach ice cream," Jenny said.

"Hildegarde can do anything, can't she, Jenny?" asked Harry.

"Just about," answered Jenny. "She once said to me, 'If you want a thing well done...do it yourself.'"

The grown-ups on the terrace were watching them. They sat there serenely smiling, just as though they were having their picture taken.

Jenny loved them so much! She belonged to them. She wanted to hug someone she felt so happy. She picked up Sam and held him in her arms.

Aunt Linda waved. Jenny knew that it was to thank her for having quieted the twins. She waved back.

"We must tell Hildegarde that she will be *very* welcome!" she said.

Sam began to bark.

"What's he barking at?" asked Harry.

Jenny patted Sam lovingly.

"Hildegarde is coming back again. Now all together...we must invite her to visit our new home. Here she is!"

"Hello, Hildegarde!"

"I wish I knew what to do for you, Sam,"
says Jenny. Her dog is really sick. His
eyes are closed, and he won't touch his food. . . .
   Jenny knows there's a strange doctor living
in the big house at the end of the street.
But does she dare ask him to help Sam?

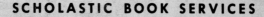

SCHOLASTIC BOOK SERVICES